BETWEEN TWO MIRRORS

"A PSYCHOLOGICAL ASSASSINATION"

by

MICHAEL J COLE

Cover illustration by Alexander Tharme-Harris Graphic Designer.
British Library Cataloguing in Publication Data
Cole, Michael

First published 2014
This book is published by
Grosvenor House Publishing Ltd
28-30 High Street, Guildford, Surrey, GU1 3EL.
www.grosvenorhousepublishing.co.uk

A CIP record for this book
is available from the British Library

ISBN 978-1-78148-717-4

International Reviews

Between Two Mirrors
A Psychological Assassination

Is the truth stranger than fiction? Perhaps, but does it seem so, solely due to our preconditioning? *Between Two Mirrors* takes the reader on a gripping journey – the age old battle between the mind and the heart. Michael Cole weaves an evocative and entertaining story in which lines that are so often blurred become defined. Or do they? A unique perspective and well worth reading. And as for blurred lines, you (the reader) get to decide.

Daya Rawat, Malibu, California, USA

If I had to describe Michael Cole's *Between Two Mirrors* in just one word, it would have to be "unique"! Of the hundreds upon hundreds of books I've read in my life, this one is in a category all by itself. It begins just like nearly every thriller – with a sense of foreboding, something out of place, a hint of danger. But where it goes from there is a place no novel I've ever read has taken me. This is a truly an unusual, wild ride.

Alan Roettinger, Author and Chef, Colorado, USA

Intervention or invasion? Sometimes sacred inspiration and at others a double take on memories of reading Messrs. Crowley, Poe, and Dante Aligieri's "Inferno" as Joel traipses through the foreboding crevices of the mind of Everyman. Unfasten your seatbelt for this ride and join Joel as he gets slam-dunked by every form of fear only to be soon again soothed, encouraged and explicitly instructed to carry on by his Impersonal Friend.

I laughed out loud at Michael Cole's knack for vitriolic self-deprecation and empathized as Joel falls for the same weary parlor tricks his fears create over and over again. No holes are barred and no embarrassments minimized as he travels through the crack house neighbourhood of his own imagination. Fact, fiction and fun! *Between Two Mirrors* reads like the autobiography peppered with honesty and humour as Joel stumbles toward a frequency strong enough to protect him from a formidable enemy – his own mind.

Joan Leahy,"Bali Independent", Denpasar, Bali, Indonesia

Between Two Mirrors moved me. I should clarify, the main character Joel nearly had me in tears.

I felt as though much of what I go through in my own life has only been validated by Joel's encounters. Best of all I gained the knowledge one is still human even after conquering one's "personality" and seeing other worlds that exists within us....

Malibu Chronicle, Malibu, USA

Between Two Mirrors is a must for anyone whose Soul has touched any form of wisdom as you are taken back and reminded of the start of your Journey. But to any Being looking for the essence of Wisdom but not quite there, these writings will take you over the top reflecting like a mirror, The Way, like a light in the darkness. Michael is a master of words. He structures sentences like the ancient Greeks carved marble. Michael makes his lines glide with concepts rich and wise like white honey flowing downward drawn by the inevitable flow of his knowledge of storytelling and the positiveness of his Seeing. *Between Two Mirrors* is an experience not to be missed, so take my advice, don't miss it.

Gypsy Dave Mills, Author and Sculptor, Phala Beach, Thailand

Michael Cole's book had me at chapter one. After reading the first sentence, I had an epiphany! "the word 'personality' comes from the Latin root 'persona' which means mask or 'that which covers the real'." I felt the heavy weight of that accrued personality that I built up over a lifetime from strategies that might make me loveable or safe or respected. I created it. It wasn't "real"! All of a sudden a huge longing came over me to clean the window and get back to the real. To get to peace and relaxation, rather than the stress of being my persona! The distinction real vs. personality is huge! Michael Cole's book is filled with these moments that if really received, could change the way you look at life – for the better!

Joan Apter, apteraromatherapy.com, Woodstock, NY, U.S.A.

Michael Cole has created the ideal stage on which Joel is able to play out his search for meaning in his life. The classic saga of the courage of the heart overcoming the demons of the ego is so skillfully told, that I found myself remembering the disappointments and experiencing the triumphs along with him. I have a sneaky suspicion that I will be dipping into *Between Two Mirrors* on many more occasions in the future.

Neil Frye, Director – CEO, Serenity Tours, Cape Town, South Africa

This excellent work of literature is presented in the most readable, memorable, and understandable form. What more could a reader ask? Well, how about "Know thyself" the Ancient Greek aphorism attributed to Socrates, the Classical Greek philosopher.

Michael Cole has captured a wonderful path to self realization in this book which will be widely and deservedly admired. This is a brilliant intellectual tapestry and a great read, enjoy!

Robin Heslop, President & CEO, Heslop Engineering Inc, Miami, USA

This book makes you ask so many questions of yourself. Once open, it's almost impossible to put down. Something hit me a few hours after finishing this book, a strange realisation that we can change our life for the better, mind over matter. The only mistake you could make with this book is to leave it on the shelf. Thank you Michael Cole – what a pleasure to read.

Loraine Donahue, Entrepreneur, Devon, United Kingdom

My golden Buddha has the smile of Mona Liza

He's as tranquil as a leopard in the snow

Bright arms akimbo shimmering robes aflow

Warming hearts with light heating all compassion

With the fire in our love

by Gypsy Dave Mills (Author & Sculptor)

Content

Introduction

"Check Cabin 21 on the way up. The key's missing from the board here!"

"Okay, okay!" Delia thought to herself. She was going to anyway. If there was one thing that rankled, it was being told how to do her job. After all she had held the position of manager of Big Bear Mountain Resort for over four years!

The moment she turned up to supervise the evening shift before she herself came off duty at 22:00 hours, she'd noticed the key wasn't hanging up behind reception where it was usually kept. She'd already made a search in the few places it might possibly be. Now she was on her way up to Cabin 12A to carry out a routine check after the last guest had just booked out, basically to make sure the place had been left as it had been found, before calling in the cleaning staff. She knew she had to hurry as there were people due the following evening. The door to the lodge slammed loudly behind her. She paused for a moment before hugging her jacket close to her to keep out the chill of the evening air. Her heart began to thump as she started the long march up the mountain trail toward the odd numbered cabins over to the south. Despite the fact that she was a fairly tough, no-nonsense kind of person, that particular walk usually unnerved her. Her fear was totally groundless, and she knew it. Nevertheless, that didn't prevent the slightly queasy feeling in her stomach and her peculiar "gulping" for air. Anywhere else around the resort and she was fine. She hadn't found an explanation for the fear and by now it was something that she had just learned to live with. She wasn't always nervous around there. In fact sometimes, depending on her mood, and the time of day, she felt a curious attraction to the place. Actually she was probably safer there than anywhere. The rangers were absolutely competent at taking care of the safety of all visitors, they had to be, Big Bear had a reputation to live up to. People came year after year and mostly consisted of families and groups of teenagers. In this case, her agitation was provoked further by the diminishing light. As she expected, a stream of nightmarish images began to tap relentlessly at the doors of her imagination. She knew that there were no "big bad bears" in the dark woods. (Despite the name, there were no actual grizzly bears inhabiting the Sequoia Forest, which made up the most part of the resort.) Nor would it be likely that there would be any desperate escaped convicts lurking around the empty cabins. She would fight off such images by humming some of her favourite songs to herself. You see, she took great pride in being considered by others as commanding a rational and down-to-earth approach to life. She was a trouper, the sort of person whom you could always depend upon and who would never let life's problems get her down. That's why she was the manager of Big Bear resort. Everyone turned to her for help, constantly relying on her strength and resilience to see them through, both in personal and professional situations. Perhaps people really did believe that she was different, and, if she was truthful, she did nothing to discourage them. It gave her a feeling of being needed, of being important. But no-one had ever sought out the vulnerable side of her personality. She would sometimes get a little weary just like everybody else. Wistfully, she would reflect that it would be really nice for her to have someone to turn to – not all the time, just occasionally, when she needed it. However, people liked to lean on her constantly and she felt that she owed it to them to be the tower of strength they thought she was, 24 hours a day, 7 days a week, 365 days a year.

As Delia approached Cabin 21, her hand automatically reached for the bunch of master keys which fitted all the cabins. Without bothering to switch on the porch light, she attempted to fit the key into the lock. She immediately felt confused. Her left hand reached out to turn on the light. That damned missing key, the mysterious absence of which had led to a certain amount of frustration all afternoon, was sitting there in the lock. Such a thing was unprecedented. She immediately adopted the attitude of an investigative officer. Abandoning all fears, she hitched up her pants, and with a set mouth and heavy frown she turned the key in the lock. There was a light left on in the bedroom.

"Okay what's going on in here?" Delia shouted, switching the kitchen and living room lights on simultaneously. She knew instinctively that no-one was present. Nevertheless, if there had been she was more than prepared. She searched the cabin thoroughly, going from room to room checking everywhere for traces of intruders, cupboards, drawers, waste paper baskets, beneath the sofas and beds. "Just like the three bears!" she thought to herself.

"Okay, Goldilocks, come on, where yer hidin'? Mummy bear's home and she's gonna find out if any porridge is missin'!"

After ascertaining that everything was in order, Delia was alerted by the wardrobe door in the bedroom that had voluntarily swung open. During her search she'd somehow missed the fact that the full length mirror, which was a standard fitting inside the wardrobes in all the cabins, had been unscrewed and removed. Glancing down, she saw the screws in a pile of dust pushed into a corner between the wardrobe and the wall. The plastic yellow butt of a screwdriver stuck out from behind the carpet's edge. She immediately conducted another, more thorough search both inside and outside the cabin which proved fruitless. Okay, so somebody has stolen a 20-dollar mirror – big deal! She had witnessed a lot of idiosyncratic behaviour by guests before. She'd deal with it later; the cabin was out of use anyhow.

It was not only people who could behave in an entirely uncharacteristic manner. "What about that sky?" she thought. Didn't it belong to some other place or some other time – like early morning, yet her watch showed 20.48 hours exactly!

She was nearing Cabin 12A, which was close to a high ridge overlooking Great Bear Lake or Lake Grizzly as everyone at the resort affectionately referred to it. It was a vast expanse of water that, if viewed from above, would roughly resemble the shape of a kidney bean. Oh yes. The sky! There was absolutely nothing wrong with it. In fact another utterly beautiful and absolutely unique sunset had fractured the sky with violent angular stripes coloured in deep harmonious shades of crimson, orange and scarlet. She decided to stop for a while and simply appreciate the beauty of it all. Strangely enough, it was up here that you always had the best view and she had very occasionally, if only to refuse to surrender to her fear, paused to watch the sun go down, leaving each trace of its departure more defiantly splendid than the last. The only explanation was that she was more tired than she thought. A moment ago, from where she stood directly facing west, she was seeing the sunrise – and she could have sworn it was no later than 5.30 a.m. A pale coral wash was invading the dark blue sky and the dawn chorus was approaching an invigorating climax.

Delia had been breathing in fresh, crisp early morning air and it had all seemed perfectly natural. She could not detect exactly when her shift in perception happened. There must be some explanation as to what she had just witnessed, but she had more practical concerns to deal with and it eluded her.

Now Cabin 12A was quite a different story. Firstly, it was a sure bet that one mystery had been solved. There, outside the cabin door, only shifted to the left to allow access, was a great cardboard box (obviously taken from the grocers back down at the lodge) stacked high with shards of glass – the broken mirror from the other cabin? Delia was grateful that the porch light was on, alerting her to the danger of possibly cutting herself on the innumerable jagged edges, some of which were quite large and stood up and out of the box like stalagmites. A myriad of tiny images reflected back and forth in an infinite number of complex patterns. It all looked quite bright and christmassy as the light from her torch ran over it. She peered into the box. Among the pieces, which ranged from one particularly tall and jagged sword shape to all the minute splinters swept up along with the general dirt, were some old denims and what looked like dirty socks and a pair of hiking boots!

"Oh God," Delia thought, "What the hell has been going on in here?" She let herself in. For a moment the woman stood there experiencing a certain degree of surprise. In contrast to the outside, the interior had been left spotless. Guests were expected to clear up to some extent, but this place had been gone through with a fine toothcomb. It was the bedroom that she was interested in and she headed straight for it. She stopped when she reached the door, alerted by a makeshift note made from a piece of cardboard and some string, which was hanging from the doorknob.

It read: "I'm sorry, but there has been an accident with a broken mirror. Most of it has been cleared and left outside. Small splinters have been trodden into the carpet. Please be careful."

Delia flipped the card over – nothing, so she just left it hanging there, opened the door and walked over to the wardrobe. The shag-pile carpet crunched under her feet. "It would have to be replaced," she thought idly as she opened the wardrobe door. What she saw in there was just what she was expecting to see and it came some way to explaining all that stuff outside. But the mystery of why on earth someone would behave like that was way beyond her imagination.

For the first time, she noticed the large white envelope which was resting on the bedside cabinet. How could she have missed that? It was stuck down and addressed to "The Manager" in fine handwriting. So, without any hesitation, she carefully tore it open. It was just as well she did because inside were five crisp, one hundred dollar bills and a short letter folded neatly in three. It read as follows:

"Please accept my sincere apologies for the damage done to your property. I assure you it was completely unintentional. I also regret the inconvenience I must have caused. I hope that the money enclosed will compensate you adequately. If not, please contact me at the following address ..."

She studied the address, pulled a face and nodded with approval. A classy neighbourhood, down in the city right near the ocean. Maybe he'd got a little drunk perhaps or – no, that didn't explain the wardrobe being the way it was. There was just one place she had overlooked: the bedside cabinet.

She sat down on the bed and looked inside. It was clean and tidy, contained a map of Big Bear resort, the mandatory copy of Gideon's Bible and a fairly thick A4 notebook with a red cover, which she automatically presumed had been left by mistake. She took it out and flipped idly through the pages. It contained chapters with headings like in a novel and occasional passages marked with dates as headings. Some of it had been written in biro with a few crossings out, the rest in pencil. It was the same clear and legible script that she'd found in the envelope and the note outside the bedroom door. She became more than a little intrigued when she saw that the name of the resort was mentioned within the draft and when she looked further she recognised descriptions of the very cabin where she was now sitting, and passages describing areas around Big Bear, like the Sequoia Forest and Lake Grizzly. She was genuinely intrigued and found parts of it irresistible reading. In fact it was so good that she could not possibly resist checking this one out. She pulled the pillows out from under the bedspread and made herself comfortable. No better place to start but at the beginning. So she began to read ....

CHAPTER ONE

The Impersonal Friend

"The word "personality" comes from the Latin root "persona" meaning, "mask" or "that which covers the real".

Quite simply, the "Impersonal" friend showed me to myself. It proved itself to be my greatest ally. It was gentle and understanding, and it was prepared to tolerate my weaknesses; yet there were times when it would confront aspects of my personality to which I held fast, even at the expense of my own growth, and that I would have pre-empted as callous and threatening. I have since come to understand that the deepest need in anybody is to be befriended, to belong. What I was shown, through my relationship with what I describe as my "Impersonal" friend, was how to belong to myself. Since the time of my first "encounter", when my friend revealed so much that had previously remained hidden, my life has changed beyond recognition.

I feel that I must describe my state of mind before these "Impersonal" encounters, as I refer to them, began. I was then living in what I could best describe as a kind of limbo, where I had no particular desires, nor ambition, with which to occupy myself. I had only just abandoned the hopes and dreams of my youth, when I had held a feeling of great optimism and power and like most of the young people I knew, considered that the world was my oyster. My problem was that I could not be bothered to dive and search for the riches I believed, and still believe, are there. Instead, I took success for granted as something that I was owed, rather than something that had to be worked for, as I have since found out. I had married young, too young, and when I lived with my family I also lived for them. I tried my best to make them happy but it seemed, to my wife anyway, that I could never do enough, no matter how hard I tried. They're gone now and for the past few years, I've been involved in the process of dismantling most of what I had been building up around myself. I have been gradually winding down and retracing my steps, until I discovered at least a fragile sense of self. I thought that in living alone, as I now did, I was protected from too much criticism. My wife and young son were "somewhere on the continent." I hadn't the vaguest notion as to where and I had reluctantly given up the hope of finding them. My wife and her family had made sure that I couldn't even if I tried. I would have only succeeded in bankrupting myself, according to my lawyers and destroying myself emotionally in the process, according to my friends. I had nearly succeeded on both counts after I had made quite desperate attempts to locate them immediately after their "disappearance". She had fallen in love with another man, although I had never been unfaithful to her and was absolutely devoted to our young child. I didn't mind losing her. After we had married she had changed beyond recognition from the loyal and loving girl I had known in our youth, to a vain, greedy, fickle woman. The "other" man was good looking, wealthy and powerful – I knew how power attracted her and, to be honest, my love for her had died. No, it was the intensely close and loving bond I shared with my son, that I had been so dramatically deprived of, which had nearly devastated me. I had never known such a love could have existed until he came into my life. I had been left an emotional cripple after he had been taken out for a “walk” with his grandmother one day and never returned. I can still remember the last words my son, then aged four, had said to me over the phone one grim afternoon: “Is that you daddy? …. Where are you? …. No-one loves me like you do. Why ….?” He was taken abruptly from the telephone at that point. I remembered the feeling of sheer horror, like I imagined the father of a kidnapped child might feel, helpless. My son will have been thirteen years old last month. Looking back, I don’t know how I had survived. At one point, I had even considered taking my own life, but I possessed a highly developed sense of survival. In time, the feeling of hopelessness and despair passed. I distracted myself in several ways until the pain, although present, became bearable. After healing myself as best as I could, and not without some initial caution, I re-entered my profession. My work offered some degree of satisfaction, and I began to concentrate on organising my lifestyle in the way which I thought would serve me best. In looking for a point of personal orientation, I discovered one important clue. There definitely was an internal journey to be made, but I did not know how to proceed. I felt as if there was a part of me that was a stranger. This produced a nagging sense of loss, which over the years led to profound loneliness. At the time, I had no idea what these feelings were that I was trying to deal with, which made me all the more frustrated. Slowly, I began to realise the importance of being honest with myself. I knew that I had to come face to face with that stranger in me, but I could not. I did not have the means to conjure that up within myself. In a metaphorical sense, I found myself reaching out a hand. I had come as far as I could on my own when the "Impersonal" friend had entered my life and grasped that outstretched hand. So, my friend came to me with more understanding of my needs than I had myself, and with impeccable timing. I look back now at how my life could have taken a different course. I might have been lured by the small ads in alternative magazines or been diverted by the public promises made by cult and religious leaders or all the intellectual crusaders of our time. All blind men offering to lead other blind men, in my opinion – the only difference being that some might possess a better public relations system than others. But that didn't happen. Something else did!

One day, sometime midweek in the early afternoon, I was sitting in my office doing some routine paperwork. My P.A. was talking on the telephone next door accompanied by the noise of the fax machine, the word processor reeling off pages from the morning's work, plus the constant tapping on the keys of two computer keyboards. The computers beside me were randomly printing out their data together with other familiar sounds: the occasional opening and shutting of doors, voices out in the corridors and the ringing of telephones. It was one of my less frantic days and I found myself staring out of the window with what I presumed a blank look on my face. For once, I was giving my mind a break from thinking. Outside, the weather could not organise itself into any kind of description and inside, my office seemed complete in its ordinariness, with its regulatory office furniture, monochromatic colour scheme and the obligatory potted plants. I heaved a sigh, lowered my head and rubbed my eyes. I could feel my heart pumping away under the influence of too much caffeine and my hands felt fat and sweaty. The first unusual thing I noticed was the excessive loudness of the 'tap-tap' of the computer keys in the offices on either side of my own. Also, I detected movement out of the corners of my eyes, as if the walls around me were made out of skin and were "breathing". The noise evaporated quite suddenly. I strained to listen. The room possessed a soundless quality. Not quiet, but literally, soundless. I could feel a steady thumping, I could not tell if it came from outside or whether it was the blood pumping through my brain. I reluctantly closed my eyes. I instinctively knew that I was awaiting the arrival of something or someone, as if there were closed doors deep inside of me which were now opening.

I took a deep breath and as I inhaled, there came a sharp ringing tone which pierced through my head, banishing all my curious thoughts which, up until now, had been busy recording all events and feelings that passed their way. As I sat quietly and calmly, drawing deep abdominal breaths instead of panting away in my excitement, I heard from some place within me a "voice" and felt an alien, yet benevolent presence, which "spoke" to me.

"I am your friend. Recognise this stillness within and around you that accompanies my arrival. Do not fear it when it comes to you again, as it will do, and soon. It is necessary to prepare you this way although you might not understand the reasons for my taking such precautions. I am neither alien nor mysterious. I am, in truth, simply a part of you, a part that has remained buried deep inside you. Remember it is important to recognise me as friendly. I intend you no harm. Also do not fear the attendant phenomena. These manifestations will induce nothing but a peaceful, even enjoyable, feeling in you. Wait for me!"

The last sentence was "whispered" almost conspiratorially. Even more suddenly than I had been drawn into this rapt state of being, I was released from it, into a barrage of sights and sounds which I was more acutely aware of in that particular moment than ever before. Everything seemed so immediate – so alive! The sun was shining, and a rather sullen almost reluctant rich, deep gold light was reflected on the wall in front of me in broad horizontal strips. The blinds rattled and were blown gently inwards by a slight salty breeze which stung my cheeks and neck with sharp, cold stabs. I was sitting in an office high up in a fairly modern skyscraper. I saw myself in caricature as I sat there in my little box, contained within a box of boxes, each with its busy little human occupant. In my mind's eye, I imagined a great honeycomb, literally a "hive of activity". Despite my assumption that I should abandon myself to sheer panic, I remained calm. It was as if I was bewitched or held in a powerful trance which retained its influence over me for the rest of the afternoon; although my thoughts were frantic in a desperate attempt to analyse the past few hours. In one brief moment my perception of reality had been completely annihilated, yet it had not shattered my composure. It wasn't until I was driving home that I started to seriously doubt my sanity. My mind desperately sought a "rational" explanation for the phenomenon I had witnessed. Despite the fact that I felt elated, I was also concerned with my well-being, although I could detect no unpleasant physiological or mental disturbance. The more I sought to mollify my thoughts, the more agitated I became. A favourite theory which I frequently returned to was that I was hallucinating due to the strain of overwork, but I found myself resisting such thoughts. I seemed to be waiting to receive an explanation. I felt sure that the entire experience was "personal". By that I mean that had anybody else been in my office at that time, they would have seen and heard nothing. The sound of the "voice" was contained within my own consciousness; it hadn't come booming out of the walls or anything. On reflection it was not so strange after all. There was always someone talking away inside my head and not always for my benefit, but this "internal visitor" had a definite identity which cut straight across my own. It had said that it would talk to me again and I was curious to know more. Despite the "strangeness" of what I had heard and felt, I could not doubt the fact that it had happened. Despite my mind's repeated attempts at troubling me, there was a place inside which "kept the faith", so to speak. I was lucky enough to recognise my doubts and hectic attempts to reach some form of "diagnosis" as merely a snowstorm in a paperweight and after a little while they settled down. I considered that it was quite rational that something I had needed and desired for so long should eventually make itself known to me and that it should describe itself as "friend", with considerable emphasis. For one thing, I had not been approached by an external agency. Just for the record, I was a confirmed cynic. Religion, whether the organised kind, or the more ambitious cults, had repeatedly and unsuccessfully made approaches throughout the years. Whatever it was that was making itself known to me belonged to no-one but myself. I don't get involved with group agreements. Also, was it not reasonable that what had just taken place back in my office should be an experience along the lines of a revelation? Do we not live for revelations of all descriptions? We read books and magazines, involve ourselves in philosophy and religion, we watch the TV and talk amongst ourselves. We want to know the truth. We want it revealed to us on all levels. Then why should I not accept something shown to me in such a way – without books, without listening to anything "outside" of me? I decided that there was nothing left for me to do but wait.

I was surprised at how soon the next "visit" took place. After driving home, I parked the car and took the elevator up to my apartment. Even as I put the key into the lock I felt an uncomfortable rippling sensation in my bowels. Was I in imminent danger? I stepped into the hall, then the dining room, switching on all the lights as I went. Everything was as I had left it. I put down my briefcase and hung up my coat. I fought off the nervous feeling as best I could and turned the television set on with the hope of orientating myself with something familiar. I plumped down into my favourite armchair and let out a long sigh. As I shifted about, in order to get comfortable, I could not fail to notice that the TV screen had remained blank. I was about to go and investigate the problem when I had an unexpected loss of muscular co-ordination and slumped helplessly back into the chair, my head lolling on my chest. My immediate thoughts were that had anyone been watching me, they would have arrived at the conclusion that I was a typical drunk. In fact I was in the grip of a pleasure, akin to relief, as all bothersome thoughts ceased to harass me. It seemed okay to give in to this simple feeling. It was something like soaking in a hot tub and relaxing aching bones, or taking a long, cool drink on a hot day. I pictured the smile on my face as that of a new born baby, relaxing in the arms of its father. A reactionary swell of fear made its approach. I could only associate it with the "friend" to whom I had so recently been introduced, which surged up inside me, eliminating all negative assertion, leaving me once again still and untroubled. The same "voice" that I had heard before spoke to me again:

"Enjoy this stillness. You are now reasonable and receptive. Do not resist what you are feeling. Listen to me. This energy you can feel defending you is a great power, the ‘impersonal’ power. I am here as a friend and a guide and my duty is to introduce you to that power. There is a part of your personality which resists me. Of course it does. It has absolutely nothing to relate to. It has been fooled into losing awareness of your life-force and so, in a sense you have been lost from yourself almost since you drew in your first, brave lungful of air. All that you have been doing recently is in preparation for this moment. I have chosen to make myself known to you because of your eagerness to understand yourself. The building up of your “personality”, or “persona”, over the years is the prime cause of your separation from the Impersonal power. However monumental the persona may become, it will possess no authority in my presence. I will teach you the skills you will need in order that you might eventually be able to experience this Impersonal energy which is your ultimate experience of self. Tomorrow I shall be here with you again. So remain open. Be prepared for anything. Don’t let fear cloud your receptivity. If you have questions, write them down and tomorrow they will be answered. Remember that fear is only a lack of faith. You have always said that you would like to know the stranger in you. Well, now you have the opportunity. I have made myself known to you. I am the friend you have been seeking.

“Make me welcome!”

Much later on in the evening when I was preparing for bed, I took the trouble to begin writing rather hurried, but accurate notes, something which eventually became a regular habit as time went on. I included all the questions I wanted to be answered. Obviously, at this stage in the game, all I had were questions. As I sat there, I discovered myself enjoying a simple childlike excitement at the prospect of developing a relationship with this “friend”. It was a bit like

Harvey, in the James Stewart movie, a secret friend or an "inner" friend – someone known only to me. I liked that. One thing bothered me more than anything else. Why was I so dominated by fear? It imposed so many limitations on what I could or could not do. After my friend had left me, the television had turned itself on and I had sat watching it for a couple of hours. The people in the news reports, the characters in the dramas, the interviewees in those harrowing documentaries; what a parade of victims! And that included all the so-called successful people. They were not exempt from fear by any means. It seemed to me that if they weren't on the ladder, they were afraid that they might never be able to reach the bottom rung; halfway up they wondered if they'd fall off. I observed a direct ratio. The higher you go, the greater the fear. Even the cartoon characters spent their time being chased by something that was trying to eat or flatten them. I would find myself identifying with the victims by default.

I could see things turning around. An agency had unexpectedly entered my life with a promise to teach me, and its first lesson, or so it had hinted, was overcoming my fears. I resolved to defeat such an enemy. I instinctively knew that firstly my fears had to be brought out into the open. I would perhaps be confronted by much that had previously remained hidden. After a lot of thinking, I fell asleep right there in my old armchair.

I awoke at close on 6 a.m. as usual, just moments before the alarm was set to go off. I had woken up in the night and crawled off to my bed half asleep. I got up and went to the bathroom. As I was shaving, I noticed my eyes twinkling back at me out of the tinted shaving mirror. I smiled at my reflection. This day held great promise. I was expectant I suppose, to the point of having butterflies in my stomach. My intuition was trying to tell me something but the answer remained elusive. I set off to work at 8.33a.m. On the way I noticed a large billboard displaying an advertisement that made me laugh. It read "Send some flowers to the stranger in your life!"

Once in my office, I kept checking the time, as I could not contain my eagerness for the promised assignation with my newly discovered "friend". I tried to relax but the anticipation only succeeded in making me more nervous than I already was. A few hours later and the same precursory soundlessness filled the room. The inside of my head felt quiet, as if I were drugged. I felt a compelling urge to close my eyes and after some initial resistance I did so. For a moment, I felt myself trying, out of habit, to resist. What was happening? My deepest instinct was to succumb, to let go, but another part of me feared and doubted and I automatically put up my defences. Inside, I entered what I, with my rather limited understanding, could only describe as a "room" within my own mind. A gentle light, coloured like the morning sky, very gradually made itself visible. So captivating was its effect that it caused my doubts and anxiety to fade away.

"Be calm and still and let me repeat that I am your friend. Let go to me. The light is there to help you. Do not let your fear reassert itself in order to determine what you may or may not experience."

At this point, I knew I had no need to resist, so I abandoned myself completely in an attempt to appreciate what was happening in all its immediacy. I couldn't honestly say that I had a complete intellectual understanding of what was being said, yet there was a much deeper part of me which I had the feeling, I already knew. It was like I had a mind beyond my mind, which was the real me. Perhaps it was the place where instinct, intuition and conscience sprang from. It certainly felt very much like it. Another rather interesting thing was that I was also observing the situation as a third person, like the cameraman in a fly-on-the-wall documentary. From this vantage point I realised that I had been manipulated by fear for most of my life. I stopped analysing and became settled, before the most incredible dialogue began.

"Welcome to my world. You yourself are part of the power which fills this place but you imagine that you are separate; I will explain why. During this encounter I will tell you much. Don't expect to be able to understand it all at once, just listen and absorb my words. That takes trust. Trusting me is all you need to proceed and succeed in your understanding. You have become divorced from your awareness of the 'Impersonal' power which you were united with before you were even 'brought into being'. Anything that is severed from its source eventually will become weak and lack direction. Its environment will seem dark and hostile. It will feel trapped. You feel that something essential is missing from your life. You don't know what it is, yet you wander around with this sense of loss, perhaps associating it with the events in your life in an attempt to understand yourself. Take your son, for example. I know you experienced profound grief over his loss and I sympathise. Now there is an empty space which was once occupied by the love you had for him. Yet think back to the time before his arrival. Were you not constantly seeking to fill that emptiness inside you even then?"

My attention was partly focused on the subtle yet hypnotic effect that the blue light (which had altered slightly as if the "sky" had clouded over leaving a softer, pearly hue) was having on my mind, enabling me to concentrate and absorb the "spoken" words. It also occurred to me that it was acting as some form of anaesthetic, because for the first time since his abduction, I felt no pain at the mention of my son. My friend did not speak for some time. I sat considering what had been said. It was all so very true and so obvious that it had never occurred to me. It was too simple, too fundamental. I think that my ego was a little offended. It sought more intricate and intellectual answers to my problems. After a while my friend resumed its monologue. It began by asking:

"You have some questions for me?"

I have no idea how, or by what mechanism, but my question on fear was lifted from me before it had begun to organise itself into any kind of thought pattern. It was no time before I began to receive answers.

"You ask me why people are haunted by fear and you rightly include yourself. Fear is one aspect of the 'persona'. From fear springs aggression, arrogance and hedonism. This type of behaviour is so rampant because men do not know their 'Impersonal' identity. Fear is basically a lack of trust, which is why I am here as a mentor to help you to understand and to relearn trust. When a baby is born, he is fresh from the Impersonal world and still acutely attuned to it. He fears nothing. He has no likes nor dislikes, save those dictated to him by his bodily requirements. He has needs but no 'personal' desires. He just 'is'. But as time goes by and he grows, the faculties of mind and intellect create a 'personality', which he starts to accept as real and absolute, not understanding that it is just a projection of thought. If an individual could stop himself from his ceaseless thinking for just a moment (and this can often occur in the more extreme events in someone's life, such as a near brush with death or a deep intoxication of some kind), he would sense this presence. As long as a man relies on his 'personality' to give him satisfaction, his situation will remain tenuous. The 'persona' is cunning! It can only maintain its existence by convincing a man that he is separate from his source, and diverting him away from anything which might provoke him to even consider its existence. It refuses steadfastly to see itself as part of the whole and uses negative thought to entangle its victim in a web of confusion. Ask yourself why your 'persona' puts up so much resistance to my presence?"

I thought about this question. Why was there a part of me which put up such a stubborn resistance to this very real and "friendly" experience? Why was I so afraid of letting go? I have had a fear of the unknown all my life. When I was a small child, I was exceptionally frightened of the dark and I also suffered from hydrophobia to quite a prohibiting degree. I vividly remember scenes of acute paranoia, when as a child I was taken along to the local swimming baths with my school friends. More than once I had run from the poolside only to be discovered quivering in the locker rooms and absolutely refusing to join in. Despite many efforts by both my parents and some of my teachers, I could not be convinced to enter the water. Eventually everyone gave up on me, and I grew up unable to swim a single stroke.

I was realising that my imagination could be used as a weapon to my disadvantage and that it was able to prevent me from venturing beyond my present situation.

"When this encounter is completed you should go to your dictionary and look up the word fear. It will state categorically that fear is anxiety caused by *real* or *possible* danger. I am certainly not a danger to your well being. I am one with the Impersonal power; I experience neither fear nor anxiety.

You, on the other hand, are plagued by imaginary fears which is why you are finding it difficult to completely relax with me. It is because this feeling is unfamiliar to you. You are like a man who has been in prison too long and when this term comes to an end and he is faced with freedom, he hangs back in terror, seeking the comfort of his old surroundings. It would be totally impossible for you to accept the situation without my help; that is why I issue effect on your breathing and distract your mind with light. You do not trust yourself and allow yourself to be constantly harassed, resulting in a build-up of angst and conflict within you. What you 'think' is happening is far removed from what is really taking place. You must learn to see that it is a game that the 'persona' plays to confuse and disrupt your equilibrium."

My intellect was stimulated and stretched itself to understand what was being said, but still everything seemed a little complicated. I came to the decision that I had little to contribute besides being a listener. I decided to remain passive.

"Whenever there is any form of power play from the persona, you must confront it. This is imperative. You have to assume command of the situation and be aware of the trickery employed by the personal powers. Understand that you are the controller. I will show you what fear really is and how it now rules over you with absolute authority. It has reduced you to a cringing slave who is sent scurrying here and there in response to its capricious, mendacious and arrogant demands. It is truly perverse and evil. It has no place in my world."

The last sentence was spoken in a soft voice yet its impact on me was as if it had been bellowed from a high mountain. The voice resumed after a strategic pause during which I was allowed to review, under a controlled situation, how pathetic my present situation really was.

"Finally, I will give you both the guidance and the tools that will permanently liberate you from fear. In truth it has absolutely no power over you. There will be a rebellion, an uprising by the 'real you' and you will turn on this enemy within and remove the usurper who has taken your crown. Then you will be in the correct position to reinstate yourself. Of course first you have to know who you are and it is my duty to reveal to you 'the Impersonal man'."

Again another short pause before the Inner friend launched into yet more dialogue, this time rapid, quick-fire information delivered in a complete monotone.

"When you admit yourself into the Impersonal world, the personal powers will lose their grip, freeing you to pursue your true purpose unhindered. Your mind, intellect and character are faculties that are built into your physical body, but their existence is not to 'control' but to 'express' the 'Impersonal' power. They are the channels through which that power can manifest its ideals, but unwittingly you have been fooled and these faculties have become wilful and have turned against you. You have invented an alternative and selfish way of behaving based on a precarious 'logic' of your own. You now have the option of behaving differently by learning the 'Impersonal' way, which would be far more rewarding. Your vision at present is considerably distorted and you are no longer conscious of your relationship with its power. The accompanying phenomena which you experience at the time of these encounters are not special effects created by Mr Spielberg, they are simply unexplored places into which I can lead you. They are places which belong exclusively to you – unique, private and complete. Your life is the journey – the territory lies within you. It is inevitable that when I visit a man within his own consciousness, the persona which has for so long reigned unchallenged, and in isolation, should feel threatened. It will summon up all of its resources in an attempt to confuse and distress him in order to make him give up. The reason for your constant frustration is that you are living your life in the dark, being consistently tricked and diverted from 'yourself'.

"I am here with you to counter that influence, to correct the anomalies in your nature and establish you firmly in this as yet unfathomed world within you. Any situation which is disorientating to the persona will cause it to draw from its vast repertoire of defence mechanisms which surround and protect it. You must not allow these powers to dictate to you anymore. It is crucial that you understand that the 'persona' is an artefact; the culmination of everything that you have encountered throughout your life from childhood, through adolescence and into adult life. It has limited powers and it must have continual and faithful support from you to grant them any potency. You are questioning my use of the word personality or persona. They are merely terms of convenience, a description of one aspect of yourself. I do not mean your personality in the way you understand the word. The word, 'persona' means 'mask' or 'that which covers the real'. Your personality, or character, is not your enemy when it lies in its proper place as a servant of the Impersonal power, but when it has become separated from its source it is like a ship without sails or rudder and becomes a slave to chaos. It thinks itself free, but it can only truly be defined as a victim. As a result the misguided and autonomous persona will make you its victim. So, when in future I refer to your 'persona', remember to take the literal definition I have just given you, 'that which covers the real'. It is that mask which I intend to remove from you during these encounters. They will eventually wear the persona down until its power is dissolved completely, then you will be left with a clear vision of who you truly are. I will not attempt to describe how that feels – instead I will leave you to experience it for yourself."

I was overcome by a sudden attack of exhaustion. I breathed a heavy sigh and let my shoulders drop. I "knew" that this encounter had concluded. I did not hear the words but my friend told me that I would be visited again. The evanescent light became what I could not describe as darkness, just "a light that could not be seen." I became aware of my body once more. My eyes were still closed. I opened them and was surprised to find myself in my office. My very first thought was to dismiss my place of work as not being a suitable setting for this encounter. I immediately became increasingly agitated as my mind conjured up selected images of venues it thought more appropriate. There were places set aside for revelations, like the open countryside or parkland surrounded by the complimentary glory of the natural world. Or perhaps a mountain-top or a cave in the Himalayas – a Buddhist monastery would be more appropriate. I had very rigid ideas about such matters. My office was, in my opinion, an environment set aside specifically for business dealings and it angered me intensely that my professional position had been undermined.

But had I not described the sensation as one of entering a "room" inside myself so why should it matter where my body was? I hadn't wasted much time plunging into an interrogation of the Impersonal friend's methods. I realised that it was the personality asserting itself, I suppose in an attempt to re-establish the territory it had so suddenly and unexpectedly lost. And I had recognised the difference. So, I had some discrimination after all, enough at least to halt a flood of doubts before they carried me away to God knows where. If, up to this point in my life I have been astride a runaway horse, then now I was pulling on the reins with all my might. I took a deep breath and a smile began to break across my face. I had the kind of feeling you have when something is absolutely right and the pleasure of understanding something for the first time. I let out a triumphant laugh.

I hurriedly pulled a notepad from my desk and began scribbling as much of the encounter as I could possibly remember. These notes, as well as the ones which followed contained many omissions, but I did my best. One thing particularly intrigued me; the mention of "Mr Spielberg". It couldn't be anyone else but Steven Spielberg whose name was virtually synonymous with special effects and to be honest the thought of some kind of sci-fi set-up had crossed my mind, Hollywood itself being "just up the road". I had a sense that whatever this power was, which was making itself known to me, already knew everything about me from the start. And I wasn't about to complain about that. It's nice to be known; to be understood. It means that you can just sit back, relax and simply be. There's no need for pretence or games of any kind. I was looking forward to developing a relationship with the part of my self that I had decided to call the Impersonal or Inner friend. I hoped that it was going to turn out to be something quite special and surprising, like a child being taken on a trip to Disneyland by their father: something exciting but safe. As events turned out I was way off target!

Later on in the day I went to a public park a few blocks away from my office to eat a late lunch. I was sitting alone on a wooden bench when I had a sudden and violent attack of nausea. I angrily pushed the food away from me and bent my head down. I gripped the bench to support myself and rocked gently to and fro. I tried taking in a few deep breaths but as soon as I thought I was calming down I would start to panic again. I was convinced that I would vomit and fought desperately hard to settle myself. I knew that I would be embarrassed if I were to be sick, right here possibly in front of passers-by. My primary concern was to avoid that potential embarrassment. My thoughts became rampant as my imagination offered me a selection of views of myself in various humiliating situations. I continued my attempt to breathe properly, but I was hyperventilating and as I tried to fight off the barrage of images that were flooding my mind, my breathing became increasingly laboured. I was gasping for breath and clawing dramatically at my throat. Finally I began to choke. I sat there coughing and spluttering with a runny nose and a face wet with tears. I began to whimper pathetically. A sudden spasm of intense pain ran upwards the full length of my spine ending at the base of my skull. It felt like an ice cold hand had gripped my head in the same irreverent way that a puppeteer would grasp a puppet and like a puppet, I felt myself being yanked upright on my seat. I was terrified and alone.

From amidst the confusion in my head there came a distinct but subtle suggestion that I should leave the park immediately. With intuitive obedience I got up and left. I groped for a handkerchief, found one and cleaned my face. Once I was up and walking, heading back to my office, I started to regain my composure. With each step, I became more relaxed as my mind began to occupy itself with the familiar sights, sounds and smells which filled the streets that led to the company building. By the time I had returned to my chair in my office I had completely recovered. An idea came to me to contact my Inner friend, although I had no knowledge of how to reach that part of me. It visited me when it pleased; I could not command it. It was no genie from a bottle!

Some fragmented dialogue from the morning encounter filtered back into my memory …. "Understand that you are the controller! …. It (fear) has reduced you to a cringing slave who is sent scurrying here and there in response to its capricious, mendacious and arrogant demands …. It has no place in my world! …. You must not allow these powers to dictate to you anymore …. The 'persona' is an artefact …. It has limited power and it must have continual and faithful support from you to grant it any potency …"

Just remembering those words filled me with a fresh resolve. It had been the Impersonal friend who had come to me in the park and had whispered to me amidst all the havoc that I had created for myself. It had come to tell me to get out of there. I had been wrong to infer that it did not respond to my desperation. It had done so in the park and had subsequently restored me to myself. If its way was subtle and gracious, then it was up to me to adjust – not the other way around. I felt grateful that in recalling the words that had been spoken to me, I found comfort and realised that I was not alone even when I thought that I was. I was able to regain control of myself. So much for my ideas – I thought it ironic that I should have such a violent reaction to my introduction to this new experience whilst sitting on a park bench in glorious sunshine surrounded by all things bright and beautiful. I had experienced sheer hell. For the first time I caught a glimpse in my mind's eye of the vastness of the amount of unlearning I would have to achieve. I felt sure that in order to correct the inconsistencies within myself, I would have to take things day by day. How precise could a man become in his thoughts and actions? Was there ever a time when he could turn around and say, "That's enough, I've accomplished all that I can now"? I had a good look at myself. I was eager to go, to climb out of the lacklustre world I had lived in for so long. I was restless; I wanted change; I wanted a challenge. With my newly acquired sense of purpose I turned my attention to the pile of papers on my desk. After all, I still had to earn a living!

CHAPTER TWO

Questions and Answers

"Primordial" is defined as that which was in existence from the beginning.
"Seed" – prime cause, beginning ... Q.E.D.

My sense of adventure was carried over to the next day. Whilst I was driving to work I had a mental picture of my son's face one Christmas morning when he woke up to a huge box of presents which I had left at the end of his bed. It was crammed full with different sized parcels, each one individually wrapped in varied brightly coloured metallic paper. He was so overwhelmed by it all that he simply burst into tears. I picked him up and held him until his sobbing had died down. I lifted one package out from the box and placed it in his hands. He became so absorbed in the unwrapping of it that he finished up spending the entire morning going through one item after another as slowly as possible. In the same way I was looking forward to the next encounter as if it were my package that was waiting there to be unwrapped. It was dawning on me just how easily I had accepted the Impersonal friend as just that; a friend. What was said and the way it felt fitted into my life like my foot in a comfortable shoe! Apart from the incident in the park I considered that my resistance was minimal. I was neither frightened nor disturbed by the sudden exposure to the "inner" voice. In the spaces between the encounters I had room to doubt but instead I felt a significant amount of enthusiasm. All I could say was that it felt good. Just that, it felt good! I drove toward my place of work in an uncharacteristic good humour.

As was my custom when driving, I reached over and switched on the radio.

"Hello….I know I have surprised you but do not worry! You will continue to drive safely. You will not come to any harm, I promise you. I can talk to you whenever I choose under any circumstances. Don't be concerned that these events will disrupt your daily life – nothing will be left unaccounted for. I have claimed your office, home and now even your car as places to meet with you and for good reason. They have become sacred to your persona because of their extreme familiarity. From now on you will come to associate these places with the Impersonal power rather than allowing them to remain cosy little refuges for your persona to work on you in between encounters. In doing this I have checkmated the personal powers for you – so you have already gained a great advantage. I will be with you later in the day."

Not only had the "inner" voice communicated with me earlier than I had expected, but from outside of me; from the rather expensive set of stereo speakers on either side of me to be exact. I fiddled with the tuner in an effort to find my local station or any station for that matter, but the radio had stopped working. It occurred to me that the channel I normally listened to was ninety-nine percent rubbish anyway. It told me absolutely nothing about myself, which to be truthful was the one subject that I was the most interested in. Then I remembered how the television had discovered that it had a mind of its own and was able to switch itself on and off at will. It had not occurred to me at the time, but it had been under my "friend's" control! I considered myself a little slow off the mark, but it was obvious that from now on, all I could expect was the unexpected.

I parked my car outside my office building, pulled my briefcase off the back seat and locked the car door. When I was eventually settled in my office, I noticed that I had just entered the building in a casual and relaxed manner, whereas I would usually rush breathlessly into the lobby each morning, dance about nervously in the lift and end up gasping for breath like a fish on land as I raced along the corridor to my office, puffing out a series of automatic "good mornings" to everybody. I must be quite a comic character in other people's eyes, I thought with a half-smile.

I became absorbed in the calm regularity of my breathing marvelling at its soothing, hypnotic rhythm. I had taken "breathing" for granted all my life, but now I was realising that not only was it sustaining that life but it was also a means by which I could, by learning to relax, become more receptive to this "voice" within me. Of course it had crossed my mind that I was going insane. Hearing voices inside your head which tell you what to do was a classic sign of schizophrenia. I had consulted several analysts in my time but I was certain that what was happening to me was not madness. If I were dreadfully wrong and it was some form of insanity, I was quite prepared to go along with it; it harmed no-one and so far I was beginning to enjoy myself. I suppose I felt a little snobbish about it. After all it was a real experience and it was happening to me. It made me feel special, chosen almost and I was the least likely candidate for such honours. I hadn't practised any kind of bizarre ritual or denied myself any worldly pleasures, like the monks and pundits who would go through agonies in an attempt to be worthy to catch sight of some particular deity or to evoke the presence of their gods. The Inner friend was just there for me undeserving as I considered myself to be and I was glad. I knew plenty of people, whom if I told about my encounters, would not only believe me without question or demands of proof, but they would also be a little envious. I decided to tell no-one. It was too personal to become the subject of either rampant enthusiasm or sarcasm and scorn.

In less than half an hour I was in position for another encounter. I was not disappointed!

"I can sense your excitement. You are eager to learn. Firstly I must make a few things clear to you. What I am describing as the 'Impersonal' power is the primordial power. The power behind every other power in existence! You are recognising that this is what you want, what you've always wanted and what you have waited a lifetime to feel."

Feelings of eager agreement flooded from me. I trusted this intelligence inside me and I wanted to let it know how welcome it was. There was a definite ripple of pleasure at my response. This surprised me and I made a mental note of it.

"Your resistance toward me has already diminished and in such a short time! A little word of warning – do not become over confident. You are still a child who has just taken your first step in the right direction. You are touching the outermost rim of this power which is able to escort you over the threshold and into the Impersonal world. If you were to experience that power in its entirety too soon and before going through the necessary preparatory steps, the psychological strain could result in your destruction.

During our initial encounter, a seed was planted inside you and each encounter which follows will provide the necessary food for its growth. It is vitally important for you to follow my instructions faithfully if you are to complete this journey. As you have already discovered, there can be violent resistance from the personal powers. They will utilise your own intellect to trick and deceive you and you must understand why. The dictatorship of your, so far unchallenged persona, is threatened by your introduction to the Impersonal power and it will become absolutely unscrupulous in its attempts to distract you from knowing your true identity.

"Like all dictators, it rules by fear. It launches harmful emotions and frustrations, and perverts the imagination as frontline distractions to unnerve you. Irrational fears are its trump card and it knows just when to use them. It knows your every weakness as it has been the root cause of them. So knowing your deepest anxieties, it will concentrate on shattering your composure. Imagination itself is not a problem – but your reaction to it is. Having said all this by means of a warning, you do have the ability to turn to me at any time. When you do, the Impersonal power will be mobilised to overcome your persona, bringing it into eventual submission. You must learn to trust me as a part of yourself and the more you trust, the more invincible you will become. As for your wanting to know when and how to contact me, that is a simple matter. It all depends on trust, trusting that I'll be there for you. Don't be surprised at the fact that all this is so basic. I cannot inhabit a nerve-wracked body gripped in terror. Your effort is merely to calm yourself. Although that in itself will not give you the means to see off an attack from a disturbed and angry persona, it *will* help.

"As you have witnessed, the persona has no power in my presence. When you know who you really are, you will be qualified to begin to direct your own life. The reason why up until now you have been a slave to your persona, is because you believe it to be, all of which you consist. All your efforts have been towards building the persona, pampering it and allowing it to broadcast its limited ideas from its unbelievably narrow perspective. You were not born to build a monument to your personality."

After a while I was returned to my "normal" environment and I began to think hard. I had become aware that there was a deep truth, a reality which I had glimpsed and recognised as a kind of "home base" inside myself – the real me and that I now had to direct all my life's efforts into reaching that point. I understood that I could never again accept the fragmented version of life that I had been living. The words of my friend came from that "home base" inside me and I instinctively knew that this was my way, my answer, my home.

I was embarking on an internal journey and knew that all my strength and resources would be required. Perhaps there would be tremendous struggles ahead of me and so much to be unlearned, and then relearned that I could only anticipate fatigue, difficulties and failure. The very thought of it tired me. Oh God, why do I have to bother with it at all! My life was running quite smoothly until all this bloody stuff started happening to me. I felt restless, fidgety and angry. Even as it began happening, I recognised a tidal wave of negativity stemming from one place, my recently usurped persona – however the influence of my encounter with my friend was too recent to be discarded and I became a man divided in two – literally a schizophrenic, with two aspects of himself in opposition to one another.

I tried to pull myself together but that merely fuelled the onslaught and I gave up immediately.

This "Impersonal" power had staked a larger claim on me than I had imagined and I could not so easily regain my old identity. I was sick and exhausted and in a state of deep disturbance. In my despair and panic I began to curse the day I took my first breath. I hadn't asked to be born into this godforsaken world anyway. Whoever started this whole mess should either put it right now or end the farce! I was feeling very sorry for myself. Tears were rolling down my face. I slumped onto my desk, my mind screaming with pain. Impersonal was a good description, no bloody feelings at all – and with no sympathy or understanding for my emotional quandary either. I thought of the happy times I had with my wife but that made me feel even worse. They weren't happy at all. They were lonely and miserable years and I'd only just recovered from the pain which had nearly destroyed me. I remembered the day "she" and that bitch of a mother of hers had kidnapped my son and that did it. I collapsed into a miserable heap and cried my heart out. After several minutes my sobbing became less intense. I lifted my head from my desk and took a deep breath. I remembered some of the words so recently spoken to me:

"It all depends on trust .... trusting that I'll be there for you.

"Why did you take so long to call me? Listen, thinking about what your persona considers to be attractive is yet one more trick in its repertoire of distractions. It bombarded you with memories of people and events that seemed to have pleased you at some time in your life. Haven't these attractive offers been a major cause of your problems and upsets. You have experienced so much grief and it was your ideas of what would make you happy that led you so confidently towards disaster. Never go backwards! Forget your memories and look forward with me. Wallowing in the past is for the weak minded who have no life in the present and nothing to look forward to. It is not glamorous; it only feeds the ego with distorted images of past adventures instigated by the personal powers. Stay with me – let me be your emotional support throughout this journey – it can only be me because I am from the Impersonal World and understand what it is you are trying to achieve."

There was a pause before my friend announced softly and introspectively:

"I have made the journey myself."

In sudden contrast my friend's dialogue took off again like a man leaping onto a galloping horse.

"Listen, as you think, so you become – look what happened to you a moment ago. Your imagination was so powerful that it made you relive pain and heartache long passed. You must always be aware of the power of thought. It is so potent that it can create an entire world for you to inhabit ranging from a pleasant dream to a terrifying nightmare. From now on, your only thoughts should be ones which you are willing to be responsible for!"

I felt reassured. I had been rescued and restored. These ups and downs seemed part of the teaching process and I was learning that, when I trusted the Impersonal friend, I felt strong and capable, yet when I let go of myself, I automatically became a victim and was utterly devastated each time. The attack upon me had seemed like the raping of my mind and emotions. I did not wish to experience that again.

"Let me remind you, that this power is a creative and positive energy. What you have just experienced was exactly as you have understood it to be – an attack. To prevent such occurrences you must learn to think and act impersonally. Give yourself room to flourish. You now possess the strength to withstand any resistance from the persona but you must remember to use it, the moment you feel panic or confusion.

"From now on we will conduct these encounters in your home. I am going to give you very definite instructions which you must follow precisely and consistently. It will be necessary for you to rise at 5 a.m., shower and refrain from eating before each encounter. Find a quiet and comfortable place that can be used regularly with no chance of disturbance or interruption. Relax, sit in a comfortable position and wait."

This encounter was now over. I must confess that I felt relieved. The role of pupil in my seat of learning had been extremely taxing and I was exhausted both mentally and physically. With a long sigh I sat back in my chair. I decided to go home earlier than usual. To try and work in my present condition would be fruitless. I realised that I had been sitting for a long time unaware of my bodily functions. I had an urgent need to relieve myself, so the first thing I did was to dash off to the Gents. I also felt unusually hungry, so I made my way to my regular lunch counter for the second time that day. I became so impatient that I stopped to buy candy and found myself cramming it into my face as I scurried along the street. This was unprecedented behaviour, but I couldn't care less. I ate the equivalent of two light meals at one sitting, returned to my office, put in an hour of paper shuffling of the most elementary kind and went straight home.

Interlude

Upstairs in the living room, the English girl's "dear sweet loo-tenant" (he was in fact a Captain in the L.A.P.D., the Los Angeles Police Department) had spread himself out on the burgundy red sofa and was beginning to drift off into a gentle half-sleep. The TV remote control was dangling from his fingers as he idly flipped from station to station, travelling through the monotonous selections on offer from both cable and satellite TV. Meanwhile the large, ground-based satellite positioned on the high and wide lawn on the south side of the house scanned the skies. Each time the viewer would decide on changing channels he would simply tap a single button on the console whilst outside the huge white dish would respond – slowly starting to shift toward the area of sky it had been commanded to search for and click heavily into place. Inside the viewer would merely see a rapidly changing display of figures which would gradually come to a standstill as the dish reached its target. His hostess had been walking in the garden and had observed it moving back and forth at regular intervals. She had deduced that either he was bored with being left with just a TV to keep him company or that he was fascinated with satellite television. She made her way to the living room to check that her guest was enjoying himself. She eyed the balloon glass which still contained the remnants of some rather fine brandy. It was the colour of dried blood and looked sickly in contrast to the deep crimson of the sofa. Fearing that the Captain's fingers might lose their grip she silently removed the glass without even touching the man's skin.

He was an old friend of her husband's and had only recently acquired his girlfriend, the one who insisted on referring to him as her "loo-tenant" simply because she was impressed by the word, rather than the bewildering way in which the English would say "leff-tenant" despite the absence of the letter "F".

Delia left the room unnoticed and went in search of her husband looking inside every room in the house – save one. She was almost creeping along, shuffling through the thick shag-pile carpet that was coloured a deep gold and green which complemented the cherry-red, satin lingerie set that she was wearing. It was only after every room in the house, including the patio that the lower gardens had been checked, that she found herself standing outside of her husband's study. The door which was usually kept locked, especially when there were people in the house, had been left slightly ajar. It swung open far enough to reveal a man sitting on a narrow bed with his back to the door, facing a giant TV screen which was flickering silently in front of him. It showed no pictures, just bright white pinpricks of light which danced before the watcher. They were large green eyes that wondered at the perfect silhouette of the man's naked torso, with its fine head covered in thick, wavy hair. The neck and shoulders were strong and muscular, but not over-developed like some of the body-builder types who paraded around the Californian beaches. A young wife was looking at her husband and simply adoring him. In an insidious snake-like movement, a hand reached out from nowhere and in the manner of an amateur stripper, waggled a large bra in the air before allowing it to drop on the bed. The man turned exhibiting a classic, well-defined profile. Without moving his head, his eyes travelled over a bulky figure which the green eyes had just noticed reclining in the shadows to the man's right. The unseen onlooker could tell that he was looking by the way the tiny pinpricks of light bounced off the edge of his eyeball. When the man's hands left his sides where they had been resting and reached out to touch the semi-naked body which had clumsily begun to uncoil itself in an attempt to be erotic, the woman outside the door quickly withdrew slowly letting out her breath and holding her hands over her face. After a while she let her hands drop. They began to repeatedly smooth down her nightgown over her hips, thighs and arms.

"Honey, are you in there? I'm just about to serve coffee upstairs."

She managed to make her voice sound calm and distant. A sudden flurry of unexplained activity sounded from inside the den before an equally calm and nonchalant voice announced:

"Just a moment dear, I'll be with you in a minute!"

This was followed by a nervous high pitched shriek, betraying the guilt which was desperately seeking sanctuary beneath a series of false, yet well-rehearsed exclamations .... "Oh darling, your dear husband and I have been enjoying the most stimulating conversation .... You're such a lucky woman! It's so refreshing to meet such a happy couple! And you know, we could have talked all night on any subject! I've had the most wonderful time! Where is my "dear sweet loo-tenant?"

The Captain's girlfriend, Angela, eventually emerged from the room to face the wife of the man she had been attempting to seduce, wearing a mask of false modesty with a bowed head and a chubby red housewife's hand clutching at the collar of a partly buttoned blouse. She was walking like somebody sliding out from the door of a sex shop, hugging the walls and refusing to look up. The fact that the wife was wearing a pair of evening shoes with at least 4 inches of heel while the other slipped by in stocking feet, grasping her tacky gold stilettoes tightly in the other pudgy red hand, created a false impression of the difference in height between the two women who both measured 5 feet 4 inches exactly. This illusion of height difference created a relative dignity that weighed heavily on the wife's side (had she but realised it). The American Captain's lady friend was hardly a girl but a woman of mature years who was also considerably less attractive than Delia, who was scrutinising her as if for the first time. The whole incident had taken her by surprise. She had trusted the Captain's girlfriend from the moment they had first met, but now Delia viewed her as pathetic and over ambitious. What would the man she called her husband, see in her? He had been drinking heavily all evening and in that state he was, to say the least, unreliable. Her female guest was drunk too but not too drunk to feel embarrassed. Driven by malice and an underdeveloped sense of self-confidence she had sought to undermine a younger, more attractive woman, presumably just to prove something to herself, regardless of the hurt she was causing. She wasn't the first and time would show that she wasn't the last, but here and now, in the present moment, it all mattered so very much.

The woman in the purple satin, whose obvious vulnerability illuminated her large, pale green eyes that held a mixture of beauty, a highly developed intellect and emotional weakness, were also an incitement to an avaricious ego.

Most people would be surprised at what thoughts were racing through the mind behind those wide green eyes.

"What a particularly pig-like face you have. You have lumpy, pink skin heaped up around your eyes, even though they're blue and you're so proud of them, but they only succeed in making you look even more like a pig. And that hair, that horrible dry and wiry hair, so full of peroxide in nasty orange streaks. I suppose you think it looks natural, as if the sun coloured it that way. All the mousy-haired girls who spend their time on the beaches near this home turn a natural blonde due to the endless months swimming and sunbathing. Poor Miss Piggy! You can't get anything right, you mean, malicious creature with your sheepish grin and your undeserved star of victory in your pig's eyes."

Despite thinking all this to herself she didn't actually have the authority to confront the other face to face, being as unsure of herself on her home ground as no wife deserved to be, and which left her thinking that everything had to be her fault anyway and that she did not possess the right to feel either pain or affront. At that moment she became literally petrified as she stood with her back to the wall and a deadpan expression on her face. The only part of her that moved was her right hand which was involuntarily tapping her hip in a strange reflex action. The arms and fingers jerked and twisted in an awkward, yet threatening manner as the voice inside her mind kept screaming out its pathetic insults, ".... you two faced cow ... you of all people ...you were treated like a friend ... you're nothing but trash, pure trash ... don't you know that you're an old hag ... he doesn't even fancy you, he's just drunk."

She carried on raging in disbelief.

"I'd like to stick the barrel of this gun in your ugly face and slowly squeeze the trigger ..."

In sudden contrast the husband came galloping out of his precious hideaway and elegantly manoeuvring himself past both women announced that he was going upstairs, "to see about that coffee." He looked straight at his wife with the eyes of a guilty man who had just been pronounced "not guilty" in a court of law.

On the bed lay an axe. Before she had time to realise what she was doing she was holding it aloft in both hands. She began to strike out at anything she could see: ornaments, pictures, a glass cabinet containing rare antique vases, a wedding photo of the happy couple. Irreplaceable manuscripts were torn to shreds, computer data destroyed, and valuable hardware pushed from its desk and smashed on the floor.

"Sergeant!"

"Yes Sir."

"Commence firing!"

The police officer stood in the centre of the shooting range facing a row of wooden cut-out targets hewn in such a way as to represent "goodies" and "baddies". She aimed and fired, aimed and fired but the wrong target took the bullet every time. What seemed like phlegm rose up into her throat forcing her to spit. She began to choke on thick, dark clots of blood - her own blood. Desperately she held her hands up to her face in an attempt to stop the flow. Each time her stomach convulsed, increasingly large amounts of blood would gush out through her mouth as if she were vomiting and spill through her fingers and race down her arms in pulsating rivulets. She knew that she was about to die and let out a series of agonising screams as her whole world turned red; bright arterial red.

Delia was shrieking and wailing when she eventually woke up, her hands covering her face with sweat trickling down between her fingers. She quickly pulled her hands away and rushed over to the windows and flung them open. There was a sudden blast of cold night air which she could almost taste. She remained standing by the window sill, taking several deep breaths and occasionally leaning out over the ledge washing her face in the black wind.

After some time she closed the windows and went and sat on the end of the bed. It had been a miserable nightmare which left her feeling sick and uncomfortable. It felt as though she could peel the clothes from her body. It didn't take her long to imagine the scenes that would be taking place, knowing that the piercing shriek which accompanied her awakening, could still be heard echoing all around the resort.

Back at the lodge, the owner and his wife would be half awake by now and wondering "What the hell was going on?" He would be rubbing his eyes and manoeuvring his great body out of bed and flinging on his old faded maroon and grey bathrobe that had shrunk during the many washes it had undergone, to reveal a pair of rather comic but ghastly knees which had become a standard joke with everyone down at the lodge. Meanwhile his nervous spouse would be hurriedly removing her hair curlers "just in case" she might be seen. The rangers too would be alerted, both those on foot patrol and their fellows, so far huddled together in their huts, would be forced to abandon their comforts of country and western music and their great flasks of coffee. They would be reaching for their torches and spilling out into the night. Their own security chief, back in Cabin 12A, was busy imagining them nervously scanning the nearby forest and what they might be expecting to find that would have been the result of a human scream. She also imagined that her cry had been carried on the wind over the mountains to the wildlife sanctuary where no tourist ever ventured, only a handful of scientists and conservationists.

Of course when Delia eventually settled down she realised that no-one outside of the bedroom where she had dozed off would have heard the distressed whimpering and the tiny half scream that hadn't quite made it into being a real yell as was so often the way with dreams. She hadn't had that particular recurring nightmare for almost a year now and it brought back vivid memories. She desperately needed to take a shower and was fortunate enough to find clean towels and a spare bathrobe, one with the Big Bear motif above the left breast.

As Delia stood beneath the cool running water she realised that she had opened something of a Pandora's box, filled with suppressed fears and emotions, things which belonged to the past and she would rather they remained there. She felt threatened and extremely uncomfortable. The disturbance could be traced back to the inheritance from a disastrous marriage, the ruins of which she had walked away from almost six years ago. She had been devastated by the loss of the only man she'd ever loved and had almost become suicidal. Had it not been for her father-in-law, a kind and impartial man whom she had been very close too even after the break-up of the marriage, she might have been tempted to "entertain that final despair". However, she did not escape from suffering almost unbearable emotional agony resulting in a long and painful illness. She couldn't eat and her lack of appetite resulted in chronic weight loss and depression. She pictured herself relentlessly harassed by demon harpies who would always manage to snatch away any crumb of happiness she might be reaching for. Consequently she had to voluntarily resign from her job, understanding that she could not accept the responsibility of being a Police Officer in her ever downward spiralling state of ill health. It was the final humiliation. Although she took the job as a security guard at Big Bear after a short break, her life was never the same. Eventually she accepted her doctor's advice and went on a course of Valium. He had urged her to take them at the start of her ordeal, but she had refused as a matter of principal preferring to battle on alone. One day during her Christmas vacation, she had staggered into the surgery disorientated and terrified. She willingly accepted the medication offered to her, as readily as a baby turns to its parent for milk. Although she considered herself beaten, the drug worked wonders and she returned to her duties in the New Year like a new woman. No-one came near to guessing what was providing her with the super strength she seemed to possess. After two years dependence on the drug and after her promotion to manager, she was called upon to "pay the piper" and so was forced to confront the addiction which inevitably escorts such medication, creeping up unawares on mostly innocent users. During the process of withdrawal which she accomplished slowly and painfully, she was as discreet as she had been when she had to disguise her impending breakdown. She would sometimes drive for miles to cash prescriptions at different drugstores, always well away from Big Bear. Most of the tiny tablets she would keep hidden, whilst leaving the others in their bottles, but replacing the labels in order that they might pass unnoticed at a quick glance as harmless Aspirin. She believed that had she been found out it would have been the end of her. Throughout the entire saga – the brave face during the divorce proceedings, the breakdown and the withdrawal from the tranquillisers; all went unnoticed by everyone around her. To summarise, Big Bear's "tower of strength" had gone through a very private hell, with no-one to confide in and no offer of friendship, support or understanding. No-one had paid attention to her then in the same way that nobody had heard her pathetic half-scream when she'd awoken earlier. But, to be fair she never advertised. Let them think that she was some kind of superwoman – it was her consolation prize.

After showering, she wrapped herself in a couple of large white towels and wandered back into the bedroom not forgetting to put on her boots to avoid cutting her feet to ribbons on the carpet. She made herself comfortable, half sitting, half lying on the bed, took up the red notebook and began reading at the point where she had left off, before she had fallen asleep ....

CHAPTER THREE

Pictures Inside the Blue Gallery

I awoke early sometime before the 4.50 a.m. alarm. I lay still in the dark with my eyes closed. I took a deep breath and at the top, in that moment of stillness between breaths, there existed the subtle fragrance of white night-flowering jasmine and I felt the delicate brush of flower petals being scattered over my forehead. It was as though masses of the creamy-white blooms had been thrown across my bed as I lay sleeping and I believed that if I opened my eyes I would see them, but I kept them closed as I lay in the garden of my half awakening. I must have fallen into a deep but brief sleep and was eventually woken by my alarm.

Within half an hour, I had already showered, dressed and made myself quite snug in the living room. The dimmer switch had been turned down as far as it could go. I went over and sat in my favourite high-backed chair, closing my eyes and lying back to rest my head. I smiled to myself thinking only a lunatic would be up at the crack of dawn like this – even in this climate.

It is impossible for something to be simultaneously gradual yet sudden, but that is the only way to describe the arrival of my friend who then proceeded to escort me into a "cathedral" within my own mind. It was fitted with a light, coloured in an indefinable shade of blue. Just for a moment I was able to detect a subtle fragrance, like the scent of flowers. The "place" reminded me of an infinite version of Rothko's Chapel; I felt the same sense of unending contemplation symbolised by colour.

"The power that was with you through the night and in the early hours of the morning was there to soothe you – to please you. It is there to help you as much as you will allow it to. Listen. This 'Original' power lives inside of you whether you are aware of it or not. It caused all life to come into existence therefore it is responsible for not only its maintenance, but also its eventual decay in order that all things 'brought into being' may return to their source. I am giving you the chance to live, aware of what is sustaining you and of having it as your reference point when dealing in human values rather than the random and incomplete philosophies which you have the option to adopt at present. You will learn that this power is what you will eventually and inevitably be answerable to. It is the seeing behind your eyes; the hearing between your ears. All of your senses are channels which are designed to unique specifications, unequalled by all the marvels manufactured by man. The Impersonal power wishes to express itself in the world it created. The sheer splendour and harmony of the natural world is a double-edged sword. It is both seductive and beautiful to mankind, whilst also confronting its collective persona. That explains why there is so little respect for a world which is, strictly speaking, only on lease. Men have become imprisoned by their freedom. They use their senses only to please and entertain themselves.

"Society has created a chaotic world which is diametrically opposed to the nature of life itself. I have given you a choice – to remain ignorant or to follow the Impersonal way and discover the truth of my words for yourself. This journey will require courage, endurance, patience and openness towards learning. Let me tell you now – you will be confronted. Your persona has collected many old habits. These ideas and concepts have become quite an effective trap – a cage whose bars have become familiar to you to the point where you have fallen in love with them. No animals could ever, ever be that stupid – but you have been."

This was pretty strong stuff, I thought, why pick on me?

"You want to know! So I am showing you exactly where you are, not where you think you are, so you might move a little more quickly. Don't get upset if your pride is wounded. Remember that I have introduced myself to you as a 'friend' and as a part of you. I will make you aware of how much you have become a creature of habit and how efficiently you have managed to imprison yourself. You must escape from this vicious circle. I will show you how to transcend your daily, monthly and yearly routines – if you are willing to admit that you have been duped."

I began to think about myself, about my character. It never occurred to me that I carried so much pride. I had gone about for a long time taking it for granted that I was a rather modest and unassuming person. It was unnerving but I knew that I would have to take a closer look at what I was composed of. I immediately became aware that when my friend spoke his words were still being met with a greater degree of resistance than I'd originally assumed. I had subconsciously tried to push such feelings aside because I felt ashamed of them, but on this path nothing could be pushed aside or buried deep enough to prevent it from surfacing eventually. It was painful to admit, but I felt embarrassed.

"It is not my fault that words have been twisted from their original meaning by humanity's collective persona. You have become cynical, and rightly so, but you must learn to discriminate. Have you or have you not decided to trust me? Listen less with your ears and try to feel what is behind the words you hear. If you start using your critique on me you will be lost. Your embarrassment is simply your own ego reacting to something greater than those things it has already mastered. Imagine that I had never made myself known to you. Where is your humility! You must treat me with respect or we will not be able to proceed."

I was left to consider for a while. I was still troubled. I didn't want to be. I thought I had understood everything I had been told and would be able to continue with this encounter with ease. It was difficult admitting it to myself, even in my thoughts, but I was becoming increasingly irritated. It was just too many words! I started to become confused because I was scared – scared to actually be angry in the presence of this "power" I was so far from understanding. Dare I be angry, was it allowed? Yet the more I tried to suppress it the more it fought to reach the surface. There was a soft whisper:

"Don't be afraid. Don't hold back or suppress anything. You must release yourself from what is bothering you."

I surprised myself as I suddenly and unexpectedly shouted out loud, "Why do you keep repeating yourself? You keep going on and on about fear, about knowing my 'true' self – all this is just basic psychology anyway. So what's new?"

I won't bother to describe the rest of my ranting, but it went on for quite a while. There were times when I thought that I had exhausted myself, only to find that there was yet more to come. Each time my feelings were less intense and more inarticulate, until my frustration – for that's what it was – had been exhausted. It was as if my mind had been vomiting and when it eventually stopped, I felt a profound sense of relief. I had an urgent need to let my friend know that I hadn't really meant one word I had said, but before I could say anything it announced:

"There is nothing to be ashamed of. You did the best thing in releasing the violent side of your persona with me present rather than harbouring such thoughts. I *will* go on repeating myself until I see that you have fully understood me. Everything I am doing is for your benefit. It doesn't matter if you recognise that fact or not. You will just have to trust."

It occurred to me how patiently I was being dealt with and I was filled with a sudden and unaccustomed humility. I felt like the incredible shrinking man whose only salvation turned out to be his acceptance of his condition. I watched the sultry deep purple which had been colouring the air around me gradually change to a soft powder blue as bright as a summer sky. I caught the subtle fragrance of flowers once more. It was jasmine; the same aroma which had filled my room as I lay asleep in my bed at dawn.

I had completely lost my underlying restlessness and was feeling perfectly relaxed. Once again the fault lay in me – not in the Impersonal friend. This time it was the problem of my perspective which needed constant adjustment. In my mind's eye I saw the print on the remote control belonging to my TV – it read: "FINE TUNE". I smiled to myself; my friend continued:

"I can show you how to change your habits like you change your clothes so that they will no longer hide your true self from you. Let me explain further. Your mind is like a mirror which reflects all the vast stores of information fed into it by your senses. Sadly, up until now, they have come under the control of your persona which can be compared to a distorted lens. Consequently, you have managed to apprehend reality and have allowed yourself to carry on convincing yourself that everything is just hunky dory when in fact it is far from being so. The result of this is that the flow of Impersonal power has become weakened and blocked. You have become dissatisfied with living in this poor condition and feel unable to distinguish right from wrong anymore. Hence your feeling of isolation and impotence. You lack power, you lack guidance. When you let go to the Impersonal power you will have your answers. I cannot give them to you in words because they cannot be given in words. In order to reach your destination you must proceed with care taking one step at a time, with me at your side always. You must learn to let go of your 'personal' ideas which build walls instead of bridges. Territory is manufactured, dispute inevitable and conflict is the result. Learn the secrets of the power inside you and you will know how to discriminate between what is real and what is not real. Understand that the Impersonal world exists by its own volition and needs no reason to do so. *It* is its own reason!"

Before the seeds of other questions and curiosities had even begun to take root, the first of these answers came to me in an unusual and entertaining manner which I viewed as if I was at the cinema. A picture formed to show a caricature of me as a small undistinguished looking man, incongruously dressed in an overcoat and hat, swimming against the tide in a great river. Finding himself overcome with confusion and panic, he manages to cling to a rock that rises up above the water which begins to flow faster and more fiercely. As he fights to keep his grasp on the wet stone he fancies that the river possesses a malicious intent – that is to dislodge him and send him tumbling with the tide toward pain and disaster. Driven by fear the man clings even tighter as an avalanche of water hurtles toward him with increasing force. He is eventually overcome by fatigue and succumbs to the more powerful element. He screams as his hands are torn away from the rock. To his surprise, he finds himself in a tranquil pool where a gentle, happily bubbling spring is tossing him into the air then catching him again before allowing him to rest on the surface, like a ping-pong ball on the top of a fountain. By now he is completely naked and has realised that he is simply being played with and that the river had not intended to harm him at all. So, he abandons his fears and decides to join in the game. My imagination continued to drift along for a while before the surface upon which the story was being told was abruptly whisked away. An intense sultry and introspective indigo light filled my head. I felt nothing. I was perfectly still and in the stillness my "inner" friend began to respond to a subject I had held a great curiosity for in the past, although it was only really a dominating interest while I was in my teens. But I had always had an open mind on the subject and, now and then, my curiosity would be reawakened by popular trends within the arts or even a snippet from a newspaper or magazine. Once again my friend's understanding of what motivated, interested or even disturbed me, was demonstrated to my great satisfaction.

"I will tell you this. There may well be other worlds inhabited by intelligent life or other dimensions, parallel universes and the like, and there may well not be – but I do not wish you to dwell on this. You have your own world to live in and come to terms with. This is the world in which you were placed. I don't want you to conceptualise anything I might say. You already have enough concepts blocking your perception of reality without your imagination being provided with any more fuel. I am teaching you to deal with your world and come to terms with yourself. Do you understand? Always turn your attention inward and continue to question yourself in these encounters. This is the beginning for you, so right now, like a child with a parent; you must place all your belief and hope with me. It is crucial, especially at this time, that you are not distracted from your goals. All you have to do is honestly desire to know who you really are, to stop pretending you are a being of no consequence and face yourself. You are now in the ball park and ready to begin the game! Should you inherit 'powers' on this journey toward becoming Impersonal (I realise that you are an inquisitive creature) you will find it impossible, should you dare to try, to manipulate them. The Impersonal can never become subservient to the strongest most highly developed ego. Should you complete your journey you will become a clear channel for the Impersonal ideals and will learn to appreciate the value of being alive. You could never use these gifts for personal gain at the expense of others. Power of this nature cannot be mastered, only surrendered to. So, you can see that this world was created for you to enjoy, care for, marvel at, delight in and respect. That is the true meaning of power, recognising your place and knowing exactly where you fit in.

"Prepare for another encounter at the same time tomorrow and remember to call me and trust that I will respond to that call should the persona attempt to interfere with you and cause you to doubt me or take up debates about what I have told you. Avoid that division which automatically occurs when you allow the persona to influence you. This encounter is now ended, I am grateful to you for paying me such close attention."

I sat still in my chair. When the evanescent light was no longer visible I felt, erroneously, that I was now outside its sanctuary and left to face the world alone. I had abandoned myself completely in this encounter and could feel the benefit of doing so, yet I felt naked and more vulnerable than at any other time in my life. My persona would be unable to defend me now, so I was forced, with my need for parentage, to turn to the Impersonal side of my nature. I felt like an adopted child – a cuckoo in a foreign nest!

I remembered a story I had been told by my grandmother whom I had been close to and had loved deeply until her peaceful death way back in my early childhood. I pictured her, a typical English rose, fading yet all the more beautiful as she was approaching the end of her own story, surrounded by pale pink roses and blue china. The story had been passed onto her by her father, my mythical great grandfather who had lived in colonial India. The story was that of an abandoned tiger cub that had been found by a small gentle doe (her own calf had been born dead) who adopted the cub and brought him up amongst the herd. They accepted him and she taught him their ways, never guessing that they were traditional enemies. The tiger grew and learnt to mew instead of roar and eat grass instead of flesh. He completely lost his identity as a tiger amongst the herd of deer and happily carried on believing himself to be one of them until one day, on the other side of a river which passed near his home he saw a magnificent tigress striding through the long grass. She was so beautiful that he stayed to watch while the rest of the herd fled to safety. The young tiger's adoptive mother remained to guard her child. She watched nervously as the two tigers moved closer together. Eventually they stood on either side of the river at its narrowest point. It was then that the young animal caught sight of his reflection and became confused when he realised that he looked exactly like the tigress opposite him. He turned and noticed for the first time how unlike his mother he was. It was at this moment that the great cat took her chance. She leapt across the water and brought down the doe killing her instantly. The tiger cub bleated in confusion and sorrow as he watched the tigress devouring her prey – but he continued to watch, his deepest instincts were awakened and he slowly began to identify with her. He automatically recognised her superior status and sat at a respectful distance. The cat wondered at this strange cub who walked and talked like the deer. She lifted her head and let out a powerful roar to show her disdain. The moment the cub heard such a tremendous sound, he too lifted his head and released his first roar. After the tigress had finished eating she retreated to her side of the river where she lay down in the grass and proceeded to groom herself, thereby granting permission to the little tiger to finish the remains of her kill. He happily helped himself to the flesh which hung from the bones of the animal he had known as his mother. It was a gruesome yet accurate metaphor for my present situation. I was beginning to listen to the "roar from across the river", yet prior to my meeting the Impersonal friend, I had looked everywhere outside of myself. I too had wandered aimlessly amongst the herd for a while – until I had accidently looked down into the river and begun to ask "who or what am I?"

It was something that everybody went through, of that I was sure, and I can remember pestering my parents when I was a small boy on every subject I can think of; such as "how did I get here?" and what was my purpose for being here. Once I remembered coming out with "what's the difference between 'here' and 'there' and 'where was there?'" It confused me now; it must have confused my parents then!

Later on in life, when I was attending university, I often took part in open discussions on "the meaning of life, the universe and what was it that one was supposed to do with it?", without satisfaction. Only a great deal of intellectual frustration, which inevitably ended up with myself and my contemporaries lampooning the entire subject quite mercilessly. Despite this attitude, I have always kept an open mind, subject to proof, and would occasionally pick up the type of religious and philosophical work that would succeed in stimulating my intellect for a short time. Sometimes they managed to inspire me but they were all so limited; like signposts! They possessed nothing tangible, relying on blind trust. I had been caught before – within the confines of my marriage. If love is blind, then so is belief. A vivid image sprang to my mind, this time from a favourite film, an adaptation of a play I had read and re-read. An invading Spanish army, for rather dubious reasons was attempting to convert an Inca king and through him, his subjects, to Catholicism. A large and fusty looking Bible was held up to a sun worshipping warrior king mounted on a palanquin supported by servants. A blazing sun lit up the whole scene. A ragged band of mercenaries stood anxiously waiting for the outcome. They were hardly able to contain their craving for wealth and recognition for which reason they had sailed to Peru with dreams of looting the great hoards of gold which belonged to the mysterious "god-king" of the Incas. Also watching the proceedings were the dark robed priests, huddled together like vultures around something not yet dead in spirit but hopefully about to become so.

The sun bounced and played off the golden skins, the iridescent feathered crown of the Inca king and brilliant scarlet robes of the unarmed Inca warriors, as if there were a relationship between the light and those who looked to it, each reflecting the glory of the other. All the native peoples from the lowliest servant to the king himself were elaborately decorated in gold which they believed to be the "tears of the sun". They had absolutely no idea of how the Spanish lusted after that metal and how vulnerable it made them. All awaited the response from the god-king. He sniffed the book, tapped it, held it to his ear and tasted it with his tongue. He was asking, "Where is your god". He could find no evidence of any "god" in the book which had been given to him, so he threw it to the ground as a sign of rejection, incidentally resulting in the slaughter of his defenceless warriors. His god had been shining on his face. He could feel its warmth and knew that his god would melt his eyes should he have the impudence to stare up at him for more than the briefest moment. And so it was with the "inner" voice, the voice of a friend who was more real to me than the sun which shone down on my face when I would take walks along the beaches near to my own home.

The qualities of the "Impersonal" friend; its gentleness, its fatherly patience, its detailed explanations and constant reassurances were impressive. I treated myself with considerably less care. I was truly a reprehensible character!

CHAPTER FOUR

A Glimpse in the Mirror

In the Oxford English Dictionary the word "authority" is defined as "to enforce obedience" and the word "slave" as "helpless victim of some dominating influence."

I arrived at work a little late after my morning encounter. It was not the encounter itself that had delayed me, in fact I had left home a little earlier than usual. There must have been some kind of incident on, or connected with, the Pacific Coast Highway because the highway patrol were out in force. They were stopping cars at random, asking to see driving licenses, checking over vehicles, interrogating drivers and other similar activities. I was one of the unlucky few – maybe my car was the wrong colour or something. I was stopped, required to produce my driving licence, questioned and generally asked to "co-operate". I had only to drive for another couple of miles before the reason for the fuss became evident. It was not the first time I had seen an accident but this one was particularly dramatic. It was obvious to me as an experienced driver that the upturned Corvette that had been smashed into a million pieces right down to the nuts and bolts and was spread across the road covering an area of about 50 yards. It had hit a stationary vehicle at high speed – and I mean 85–90 miles an hour – almost double the legal speed limit. There were tyres, pieces of fibreglass – just about every part of the car had been thrown in all directions. I knew that whoever had been in that upturned Stingray must be dead. I also guessed that the accident had been the result of a high speed chase, judging by the police presence. I drove on in a mild state of shock. That was the one thing which you could guarantee would happen to you in your life – that you would die one day – and that day would not be found written on your Birth Certificate! I recalled reading about Castaneda and his experience amongst the Yaqui Indians and how his teacher, an old and powerful sorcerer, had taught him the importance of being constantly aware of his mortality. In my case, it had taken the witnessing of something as graphic as that accident back there to remind me that it could happen to me at any time. I think a lot of people drove to work more carefully that morning.

The whole incident plus the traffic diversion had succeeded in making me late for an important meeting. My business partner (and senior) had never come down quite so heavy about my being late before despite the fact that it was totally unavoidable. I honestly thought that our contract was on the line. He made me feel like a clerk. He was in a terrible mood because he jumped on my back and stayed there throughout the morning. I felt the full weight of his authority and ended up having quite a distressing day. When I got home, I headed straight for the bar and poured myself a large whisky. Just to make matters worse, the bills had arrived that morning. The first two that I opened contained enough gloom for one man in one day so I didn't bother with the rest. I became thoroughly depressed, dismissed the whole day as just bad luck and went to bed early.

I had a disturbed night's sleep beleaguered by dreams and spent most of the time getting up and making cups of tea every two hours or so. I thought about how the time spent in the company of the Impersonal friend had become increasingly important to me. It was many things, among them an opportunity to escape from the mundane, almost Kafkaesque view I held about my business and social life. I remember reading *Metamorphosis* and how, after Gregor had turned into an insect, I expected some miraculous change to happen in his bleak life. I confidently read on, hoping that of course he would change into a beautiful butterfly and make his escape into a new and beautiful world. But he didn't – he just died! Imagine my adolescent disappointment. I didn't read much of Kafka after that.

During my life as a businessman, I saw myself living like a hamster, going nowhere fast on one of those wheels (my son had kept one as a pet). I've seen the look on those stupid creatures' faces when they dismount only to find themselves back where they started, sitting in front of the same little bowl of sunflower seeds. Poor things, I bet they thought they'd made a real getaway. When my silent grumbling had subsided, I felt some deep inner restlessness. I stayed awake from about 4 o'clock waiting for the dawn and another encounter so that I would have a chance to deal with all the questions which were bothering me. (It seemed to me that all I consisted of were questions.) My disturbance was coming from deep in my guts, that place where you feel anguish or pain. It was an emotional concern that was surfacing to be dealt with and I knew it was serious. I felt tears rolling down my cheeks. They continued to slip away over my chin and trickled down underneath my shirt making my tummy slightly wet. I must have been weeping a great deal – silent, solemn tears that I didn't bother to choke back. I don't know for how long I had been sitting there weeping, but eventually the time came when my morning's encounter had begun. By that time, I was consumed by the essence of my question which was in plain language:

"Why does this Impersonal whatever, who shows so much kindness and consideration to me, allow the simple people, innocent creatures and the irreplaceable environment, to suffer in the hands of the greedy and powerful?"

To me it was outrageous that it was allowed to occur.

"Most people ask that question at some time in their lives. Very few get an answer that satisfies them. Unlike the animal population, human beings are able to turn to their gods and ask 'Why are you allowing this to happen?' Don't think for one moment that that's because animals are stupid. That is far from the case. Never underestimate them, ever!"

I remembered the hamster and became a little embarrassed. I started to justify myself by thinking that of course I had only been using the example of the hamster as a kind of metaphor and anyway it was all done in such a light-hearted manner, but I found that I couldn't con myself, not with my friend right there knowing what I thought about and the way I thought about things. The simple truth was that I was an arrogant bastard. Despite me passing judgement and sentencing myself to feel a certain amount of shame, my friend carried on.

"It seems that you too must have the answer so that you may be confident enough to trust in the Impersonal power. As I have explained to you, all that you are surrounded by and live with in this world is 'bought into being' by the Impersonal power. Its ideals are not affected by the actions of mankind. It carries on sustaining all that it is responsible for regardless of conduct. It is not the ultimate judge whom men have invented in many forms that will punish the wicked and reward the good. The Impersonal power has been appropriately named; it serves the good, the bad and the ugly and leaves them to find the best way to live. The judge that humanity seeks here, there and everywhere sits inside him. However its voice is so quiet that it is, more often than not, drowned out by the screaming in this artificial and pretentious society which exists at present. People still argue, fight, pollute, dishonour, violate and destroy, but the Impersonal power cannot be anything but what it is, a constant outpouring of positive energy. If people continue to avoid the truth, they will remain distraught, desperate and weak-minded. They have already become prey to their collective persona which they have manufactured and allowed to rule in a wilful world of their own making. The consequence of this ignorance of the dictates of the Impersonal ideals are that men have revoked their privileges, the privileges of knowing who they are and what they are meant to be doing once they have received the gift of being 'brought into being'. It is up to man to be honest with himself."

I felt confused by the word "Impersonal". Was it a state of being, a vision, an intellectual understanding?

"It is merely a term of convenience. I use it to describe the indescribable. When you encounter what I am loosely referring to as Impersonal, you might well find another more fitting term to employ. It is entirely up to you. My best advice to you is to remain in the present and consider yourself a pupil who must sit in the classroom and listen to his teacher before he can run out into the world and play."

There was a pause where I assumed that the Impersonal friend was assessing my readiness to keep my thoughts still and listen. Then it continued:

"I want to tell you something else. It is possible that this 'Original' power might grow impatient watching mankind's efforts to control their own destiny. Consequently, inside everyone there is a power struggle going on. Mankind will only find rest when people take responsibility for their lives and let go to the Impersonal side of their nature, to become positive, harmonious and happy creatures. This will only become possible if they cease to continue to believe themselves separate from their source. The opportunity I am giving you is a chance to end that imaginary separation. Nothing can remain separate from its source unless it is able to 'think' that it is. Only humans have that rather dubious ability. The more you learn to exercise control over your wayward persona the closer you will become to being reunited with yourself. There will be no more struggling with your ego which has dominated you for your entire life. Now at least you'll know that there is another part of you to turn to, which will not let you down.

"I have some simple instructions for you to carry out before the next encounter. You may call it your 'reflection' or 'mirror' technique if you like. It is an elementary exercise involving nothing more complicated than sitting in front of a mirror, making sure you are comfortable and studying your reflection. Look closely at your face, your body, hands etc. See them as parts of a machine which you inhabit. Understand that neither did you create, nor choose the vehicle which you are using – it is a rare gift, to be 'brought into being'. Consider yourself a caretaker rather than the owner of a thing so precious. You have a choice. Allow your body to be at the beck and call of your persona or become a servant of the Impersonal power. You flinch at the word 'servant'. Have you not heard the expression 'My servant and the better man?' Besides, you are already unfortunate enough to be nothing but a slave. Consider the difference between the two. A servant voluntarily enters into a contract with his master to perform a specific duty and receives protection, payment, even love in return. On the other hand a slave receives no reward, no respect, and no hope."

There was a pause. It seemed to be some time before my friend continued.

"By allowing your persona free rein for so long, you have come to identify with your body as being the sum total of what you consider yourself to be. This exercise is a method by which you can begin to free yourself from some of the limitations which have been placed upon you. Perhaps your body is tired and exhausted by the stress caused it by having to perform actions whose origin has stemmed from negative thoughts. Entirely personal actions will always cause your body undeserved stress. You must look into your eyes and feel that you are the life and only the 'life', the 'eye' witness, which stares out of them. You must learn to make this distinction."

These instructions seemed simple enough, but something was troubling me. I was concerned about my life. The day before had made me aware that I was not alone in the world with complete autonomy over my situation. The police had stopped me on the highway and made me late for my appointment. My livelihood was dependent on the whims of my superior. I was anxious. Would I be able to keep the material side of my life running smoothly now that I was embarking on a journey which seemed solely concerned with, for the want of a better word, the "metaphysical" side of things.

"First you must recognise authority for what it is. You have encountered social authority, which is authority outside of yourself. That, I promise you, is not your problem. Your problem is who is in control, your persona or the Impersonal power. Who have you voted into office? There is, whether it is a good thing or not, a democracy inside you and you have the right to choose which part of you will govern your life. What you see as authority outside of you can be dealt with simply. Although your society is by no means perfect, you must humour it in order to keep yourself free from trouble. You should keep a low profile at all times so as to retain your privacy and do not seek to elevate yourself socially, that is a waste of time. The right to earn a dignified living is the right of all those 'brought into being'. Learn to walk along the path of least resistance. You must tread carefully throughout the minefield of rights and wrongs which differ so radically from culture to culture. On your way through the world you will cause no harm to anyone and you will live in such a way that no-one will want to cause you harm. Inside of you, you will never feel alone. Now this encounter is over. Remember that your real work is in front of you. It is essential that you do your reflection exercise in order to prepare yourself for the next step on your journey. I will be with you again tomorrow for another encounter. My guidance and influence are always there to call upon. I believe that you have already experienced my proximity and my readiness to help you. Should you have difficulties just remember which part of you to turn to and which part has the means to help you."

The encounter ended. I sat and wrote some notes before leaving for work. Later that evening, once I was settled in my home, I was confronted by the task set for me – the reflection exercise. I thought about it for a while, what it meant and the effect it might have upon me. I sat attempting to understand the mechanics of it all, but I merely succeeded in blanketing the situation with wild imaginings. I could not resist the temptation to personalise everything. Then I remembered I had been instructed to "do" the technique, not sit thinking about it. I had allowed my mind to wander over everything like a disorientated spider that would be more than likely, catch himself in his own web.

After some wasted time, I got up and went looking around for the best possible site to begin. I realised that my first duty was to make myself comfortable. I had not changed my clothes, which were beginning to feel like a strait-jacket by now, so I would take a cool shower and change into some loose cotton clothes. I also decided not to have any food as a full stomach would tire me and make me lethargic for the rest of the evening. Eventually, I decided to use the large bedroom mirror. It was full-length and gave a clear reflection. Incidentally, it was the same mirror I would consult for a final assessment before going out of my front door to face the world. I pulled a chair over and sat down. Once I was in a comfortable position, I looked straight up at my reflection. I found myself regarding my appearance in a way in which I had never done before. The person I had looked at so many times was a total stranger – someone about whom I knew nothing. I began to take note of my face, my hair, the way my clothes hung from my body, the folds in the cloth, the way my hands rested upon my lap. I was studying a portrait of myself! An image as unlike me as a photograph of someone is unlike the true subject. He lives, breathes, walks, talks, loves, hates, thinks, grows, changes and dies. The image, whether it be a painting, a snapshot or a sculpture can outlast his life for years, decades even centuries. There was my form, my human body and my life. I was starting to understand the difference.

I could feel my hair standing on end!

A nervous spasm started at my feet and travelled upwards all the way to the crown of my head. It felt as if I had a hat on. Whilst I experienced, my mirror image did not. As I continued to focus on my reflection, the more concentrated I became and so my experience intensified. Fleeting thoughts were attempting to distract me. For the first time, *I* consciously commanded my "persona" to be still and as I did so, I felt some part of me connected to that command, banish all thought, leaving *me* alone and undisturbed. My face looked as if sunlight had been spread across it. My breath sank with something like a heavy sigh as I exhaled deeply, probably because I was starting to relax. I waited to draw breath but I seemed to be suspended in "the place between breaths" for a short while until my fear of not being able to inhale had subsided. I had felt intensely afraid at one point and actually thought that I had been dying. The place where I now know was panic, was not able to hold me in its grip and so I relaxed. The minute I did so, I was drawn inexorably into a whirlpool of power that rotated with incredible force and attraction immediately beneath me. I hesitated for a moment before I felt a total acceptance of my fate. At that moment, I was pulled down into the vortex. It seemed as though the Impersonal power had taken the shape of a human hand; a soft gentle hand like the hand of a young baby or the silky hands of my grandmother. I was caressed and stroked, not my physical body but the "me" that lives inside that body - the "me" I had identified in the mirror. It was important that I understood which part of me was being loved and played with. After a time that could not be measured, I was lifted up and out into the exhilaration of inhaling. What joy; what a unique privilege to be able to draw breath, to be invited into the arena of life one more time. It was as if those hands had lifted me up and into life because they loved the life within me; not my character, not my history, not even my potential. The same raw energy that had drawn me into the vortex was spiralling around me like a tornado, strung together in a coil as real as the muscles of a boa-constrictor. I was being lifted up into the eye of the whirlwind. Although I could see nothing I imagined that if I reached out with my hands I would be able to feel the tension in the air.

All of a sudden I became Dorothy being whisked away to Munchkin Land by a twister; "Follow the yellow brick road, follow the yellow brick road. We're off to see the wizard, the wonderful wizard of Oz, because, because, because, because – because of the wonderful things he does!"

My breath fell again and I plummeted down into a great silver pool, down beneath its surface where I began to float around in a strange, cold heavy liquid. "It's mercury," I thought and became excited because according to my birth sign, it was the name of my guiding planet as well as my lucky metal. Once again I was surrounded by a perfect and complete stillness. I knew that, had I wanted to, I would not have been able to move at all. All movement down to the slightest twitch of a cell wall or the delicate sway of any cilia, had come to a complete halt in order for some miraculous organic process to take place. I could still detect a packet of energy gently circulating around me as I drifted like a foetus floating in its own embryonic fluid. I had curled up into a ball; even my fingers were turned inwards. Contained within the swirling liquid-solid were minute seeds which began dislodging themselves, one by one, from their calculated revolution around me before launching themselves into an orbit around my mid-section. Imperceptibly they found a way into my body where they proceeded to hide themselves lying dormant as if sleeping under winter snows.

I looked at my reflection again. I sat calmly with a smile on my face. A fleeting thought crossed my mind that perhaps my reflection and myself had a separate existence and that it too was sitting watching me, but I did not bother to pursue the idea any further.

I sat for a long time, barely drawing breath waiting for the completion of what seemed like some kind of fertilization process until I could no longer sense the invasion of my biological and molecular being. In that moment, I grasped the idea that I was “female”, in the sense that I was by nature a passive creature; a receiver of power and understanding, rather than a manipulating and dominating force. It was a fleeting vision, but one that would stay with me for the rest of my life. I managed to sleep, a light half-sleep, and when I awoke I could not help but look up into the mirror again. I could not distinguish between the reflection and myself. It shocked me and I began to think hard in order to regain a sense of reality. I remembered the story of the Chinese sage who dreamt he was a butterfly and when he woke up he began to wonder if he was a butterfly dreaming of being a man. I fell into a bit of a trance sitting there for what seemed like hours, thinking about the story over and over. There was an invasion of other less welcome images filling me with doubt and insecurity. What or whom was I now? The friend within had lied. It was trying to destroy me. How would I be able to live, to survive, with all these strange goings on? I’d be late for work.

“Quick get up, you’ll be late for work!”

I jumped from my chair, almost knocking it over.

“Don’t look in the mirror, it’s a trick – it will get you.” I ran into the living room where I began turning everything on; the TV, radio, the lights and subconsciously avoiding any reflective surfaces, headed for the bar. I stopped and leaned against it, wet with perspiration and trembling from head to foot. I began shaking so violently that I could hear my teeth and bones rattling. "Oh my god," I thought, "I'm going to fall apart." What a noise. My breathing was so erratic that before I could even raise a glass to my lips, I began to choke and cough. At one point I thought that I would die. "I'm going to die. It's trying to kill me. These strange powers are trying to kill me." I fought to control my breathing but from such a point of panic that I was only making things worse. At that moment, from the pit of my stomach, I felt a gentle trickle of warmth which began to reach upwards grabbing at my throat and filling it with a kind of fiery liquid, not unlike a shot of brandy (at that very time I was pouring a glass of Courvoisier, most of which was spilling over the sides of the glass) until I returned to normal. The fear vanished, scuttling away sideways like a crab into whatever dark corner it had been lurking. I watched its retreat with disdain and disgust. "I mustn't let that filthy thing near me again," I thought. I had been weak, allowing myself to be caught like that after sleeping. I had not been told to fall asleep. I felt bloody stupid. Only this benevolent power which I was drinking in breath by breath, had rescued me from it, as it was busy trying to strangle the life out of me over by the bar, meanwhile telling me that the rattle of glasses and bottles were my bones. I felt it necessary to return to the bedroom in order to complete the reflection exercise to my satisfaction. I had been having the most powerful realisation, the intensity of which had diminished only so that I might rest a little before going on and in that single moment, I had been caught unawares. I had to remain on my guard at all times against the persona now I had the eyes to see it for what it was – my greatest enemy. What was truly disgusting and absolutely horrific was that I allowed it to live inside me – like a vile parasite. I remembered a documentary on tigers. A cub had been injured. Through the open wound on its leg, the parasites had entered and eaten the poor creature alive. It had suffered and died. I remembered crying. It was so weak and defenceless. Its mother had deserted it. My parentage was self-contained, built in. I was answerable to myself only. When I thought about it, it was the perfect solution. I was responsible for my own actions – there was nowhere to apportion blame. The age when my parents were considered to be responsible for me had long passed. In fact I was a father myself. I couldn't hold the state, or society or my upbringing responsible for what I would do with my life. I was alone; with my own voice of conscience which demanded that I listen to it and follow its instructions. I was being policed by myself; I could only commit a felony against my "self"; I even had the greatest agent to be responsible for my punishment – my persona.

I sat down in front of the bedroom mirror exactly as I had done before so that I could see the exercise through to its conclusion without any interference. I felt comfortable with all personal confusions held at bay. "There's a part of me, which knows precisely what to do," I thought, "and it's taking over." I looked in the mirror and as my eyes met, the sparkle on them began to expand and give off a warm radiance. I felt at home with myself although this time there was no great activity as there had been previously. I was changed but not traumatised by what I now knew about myself. It was as though I had been on an operating table and I had tried to get up while my insides were exposed and the surgeon had a chance to sew me up. That's why I had fallen victim to the personal powers. I had to let these encounters run their course no matter what. I would certainly remember that in future. Meanwhile, I lay basking in a warm internal glow which felt like the sun shining on my soul. Having lost all physical sensations, I was aware only of the seeds of the Impersonal power which had taken root inside me before attempting a gentle re-entry into the atmosphere of a living world.

I was touching life! Never before had I encountered such a sublime and exquisite joy. Not since I had become aware that there was such a dangerous division within myself had the fact that I was not the deadly and subtle persona I had developed over the years been so vividly demonstrated. I was an autonomous energy unaffected by anything that existed outside of itself.

A spine-chilling thought struck me dead centre. How had I lived without this understanding for so long? I smiled to myself understanding why I had been through so many traumas in my life and why from time to time great battles had raged inside my head. I had no point of authority to turn to, to ask what to do, think or say. My persona, which was just so many fragments of other people's ideas, was certainly not qualified to lead me to a point of equanimity or even hint at the right direction, yet it had successfully managed to make innumerable yet futile attempts to distract me from realising my full potential. Like the sun worshipping Inca king, I could not accept the words in any book written by a man, (even though I might well agree and attempt to utilise the ideals I discovered in them). All my life I had never met that which had absolute authority over me. – power, yes: authority, no. I had accepted the authority of the Impersonal power over me and it felt good. I had been given a reference point which was constant and would always be there to back me up when I lost my way – and why not? Was I created to be abandoned? It was only logical that if the effort to “bring me into being” had been made, it was not so that I should be ignored. The decision was made to befriend and guide, to protect and reveal, to confront and comfort. The Impersonal was all this to me. What was also important to me was that I had found a solution to one of my biggest problems.

“Face yourself then, face the world!”

I eventually managed to pour that glass of brandy, wrote some notes and retired to bed.

CHAPTER FIVE

Window on a World

"Because today is the beginning of your vacation, I expect you to take advantage of the time you have to concentrate on your encounters with the Impersonal power. Since you have been introduced to the reflection technique, you are now able to recognize that there is so much more that has gone into your 'bringing into being' than you could ever have imagined. Once again I will warn you not to relax your guard against the ever resourceful and cunning persona. It has lost much ground since that day in your office when you felt the doors to your Impersonal self open and I offered my hand in friendship. The more it is pushed into a corner the more desperate its attempts to distract you from your chosen course will become. You have witnessed its subtlety and its malice time and time again. Now you can see where the cause of all your miseries has come from. Inside you lies your greatest enemy and also your most loyal champion. Obey the voice of reason; after all it has invested both time and love in you. The persona has been cornered. It sees my power. It will become more and more desperate. It will stop at nothing to survive. Also, it is so possessive that it would rather you die than witness your entrance into the Impersonal world. Therefore the only option left open to it is to destroy your trust. It is likely to provoke you into regrettable actions and then blame their consequences on me. At this moment, it would be disastrous if you were to turn away from me. I am both your refuge and the way forward. I cannot sit by and allow you to hurt yourself, so I am strict and watchful. It is no easy task you have undertaken, however that is no reason for you to doubt yourself; that would automatically put you under the rule of the persona. Remember this: the personal and the 'Impersonal' cannot take up residence within you at the same time, so you must choose your guests wisely. Take the rule that two things cannot exist in the same space at the same time as an example, to make it clear to you why you must let go completely and become Impersonal. There is as much difference in the two states of being as there is between life and death."

I did not feel confident at all. Did I stand a chance against the persona should it decide to throw itself against me in a desperate attack? After all, it was fighting for its life.

"So are you. Remember that."

But it was cunning, it had seduced me before and to be honest I had enjoyed abandoning myself to it. I felt confused and unsure of myself. What was it – what part of me enjoys being taken for a ride? A short story by Edgar Allan Poe came to mind. I had been particularly struck by it when I'd first read it and each time I re-read it, it never lost its impact. It was the story of a young man who speaks to the reader from a prison cell explaining how he had arrived there waiting for his death at the end of a rope. Although he led a perfectly content life, perverse thoughts began to enter his mind suggesting that he murder his benefactor both for the pleasure of committing the perfect crime as well as benefitting financially. So overwhelming was the temptation to do this thing that the crime was eventually carried out. The youth inherited everything and no cloud of suspicion ever passed over him. For years he was happy with his accomplishment until one day while he was taking a walk he again became overwhelmed by the perverse temptation that, after all this time, he should confess his crime. The compulsion to do so became unbearable not to obey. In the end he surrendered to this perversity and began to run down a crowded street screaming and shouting his guilty secret so loudly and so insistently that he was arrested, tried and sentenced to be executed. The title of the story was *The Imp of the Perverse*. I felt that just such a creature lived within me. A typical example of the power it had over me, was when it would urge me to drink too much against my better judgement, then derive further pleasure when I was left with a hangover the next day. What really infuriated me was the fact that I harboured this perversity which would continually prompt me to perform these actions promising me that I would benefit. I never did, for after the deed was done, I would invariably punish myself relentlessly by wallowing in guilt and remorse no matter how trivial the offence. This perversity within had made me its whipping boy and it was still there playing the same stupid game, only this time the stakes were higher and increasing day by day. How could I free myself? The reply was swift.

"Don't listen to it and do not fear it. I have advised you to be watchful and cautious but there is no need to abandon yourself to terror. Even now it has convinced you that it is indispensable and that it holds a greater power over you than is actually the case. It constantly menaces you, causing you to feel unsure of yourself and unnecessarily vulnerable. I will make a promise to you. We will win through together because, whatever it throws at us, makes us stronger. This seductive power, which appears to hold such pleasure in its hand and is so 'kind' to you when it has a grip over you and is not threatened, will always be uncertain in my presence. Are you familiar with that game? Paper covers stone, stone blunts knife, knife cuts paper. When I play that game with the personal powers, dare they get that close to me, I always, without exception win. Defeat is unknown to me."

So I was championed by my "Impersonal" friend. I was not alone to face all the bug-eyed monsters that were ready to pop out the bag. I began to feel a little more confident. There were problems, but nothing that could not be dealt with.

"The more you become Impersonal, the more impregnable you will become. The persona will find it increasingly difficult to deceive you. It will be left looking for the tiniest cracks and crannies through which it will attempt to inject fear, but you must constantly be on your guard letting your realisation of who 'you' are be an unassailable fortress. Remember the saying, 'knowledge is power'. Never judge a situation by the results of a previous situation, for in doing so you put a limit on the potential of the present situation. That is a habit of the persona, whose whole aspiration is to build walls around you as it can only survive in a limited space. It likes to be a big frog in a small pond. It can be patient too, waiting for the chance to catch and play with you, like a cat with a mouse. Remember that it was never intended that you find your way into the Impersonal world without help. When this encounter is over you will be left with a choice, either to respond to the suggestions I have given you, or falter and succumb to doubt and procrastination. If you fail to abandon yourself completely you will be caught in the middle of a struggle with the persona. You've been caught like that before and I know you did not enjoy it. Luckily you have come far enough, to recognise the

'Impersonal' power when it comes to bail you out of whatever uncomfortable situation you might find yourself in. So I have told you what to do and I have given you sound advice. What you make of your day is up to you!"

For the first time I thought about the day which was stretching out before me. Twenty four hours was a long time. I have always taken it for granted that there would always be more days to follow. It was just something that I had done unconsciously all my life. I had wasted time like I'd wasted money, and ironically it was always the loss of money which I considered to be the more painful. Again I remembered a little story, one which a priest had told me when I (due to my parents' wishes) had been forced to attend Sunday school, which demonstrated exactly what I was up against. To this day, I can vividly remember his exact tone of voice and the particularly flamboyant gestures he would use to keep the attention of a bunch of rather unruly kids who would rather have been outside playing cowboys and indians in the cemetery. The story went as follows: one day a saviour came to earth, gathered some disciples around him and began teaching them how to become good and holy men so that they could all go to heaven when they died. (I'm repeating the story in the same quaint, slightly patronising way in which it was told). Down in hell, the devil was so furious that he called all his demons together, chose one of the most evil and sent him up to earth to stop everyone becoming disciples. After a while, the demon returned to hell in order to report to the devil that he had failed in his task. He explained that although he went among the people and told them that the saviour was a fake, they did not listen to him and chose to remain believers instead. The devil became angry and killed his servant on the spot. Then he called for his chief demon, upon whom he always relied to do a good job and ordered him up to earth to see what he could do. After a while he returned and told his story. In order to gain everyone's confidence he had at first pretended to be a disciple himself and had even become quite adept at mimicking piety and devotion. Slowly, he began to preach, eventually proclaiming himself to be the saviour. At first, one or two disciples were fooled, but after a while they saw through him and returned to the true saviour, begging forgiveness. His cover blown, the chief demon had rushed back to Hell to escape retribution. However, the devil was even less charitable than expected and with one breath reduced him to ashes. Then the devil announced to the citizens of Hell that, since the job was so important, he would have to do it himself "as usual" and went up to earth to prevent the salvation of mankind. He was back in less than one day full of self-congratulation. Amazed by the speed in which he had accomplished his task, all the denizens of Hell gathered around him, begging him to tell them how he'd managed to defeat the saviour and disillusion his followers. He replied, "It was easy. Firstly I became a disciple myself and began by praising – you know, 'Him'. Secondly I told them that it was wonderful that they had been revealed the path to salvation, that they should definitely pursue it and then…" (The devil paused for theatrical effect), in the following hush he leant forward and whispered – "I told them to take it easy as they had plenty of time!"

In the story I referred to earlier on in my notes, *The Imp of the Perverse*, procrastination was described as one of the most insidious manifestations of perversity and I found that simple little parable quite frightening. My tendency to take my life for granted was frightening. I thought about the car accident I had witnessed just a few days before and shuddered. There was a popular saying which summed up my mood; it went, “Welcome to the first day of the rest of your life.”

I always felt a little disorientated when I would break from work. I needed a little time to adjust to having nothing of any so-called importance to do. I was a little disconcerted after analysing that my disorientation was due to the fact that for the time being, my identity as a “businessman” and “entrepreneur” had been removed. I remembered returning home the previous day and removing my custom-made Italian suit, carefully placing it on its broad padded hanger, pulling off my silk tie (which matched the lining of my jacket) and throwing my Dior shirt into the laundry basket. At that point I was both literally and symbolically naked. Like the proverbial snail removed from his shell, I was in relation to no-one and manipulator of no “thing” or “concept”. Today I didn’t have to hang around half the morning pampering the knot in my tie. I took a long hard look at myself. Was I really held together by paper clips and staples? Did I walk around broadcasting my thoughts like a fax machine? Was part of my life’s philosophy “I work, therefore I am”? Did my sense of self-worth increase and decrease along with my bank balance? I decided to call my daily and tell her to take a couple of weeks off (with pay) and spent the morning doing housework and preparing food. I found it to be a relaxing, even pleasant, task. After I had eaten lunch and taken a nap, I had nothing to do except sit down and perform the mirror technique once more. I reflected for a moment about how my life was being pared down to essentials and how these “encounters” were, without doubt, the focus of my day. I eased myself down in front of the bedroom mirror, bowed my head to relax my neck and allowed my shoulders to go limp. I was nervous in case what I had experienced the day before might repeat itself, so I was careful not to fall asleep. To my surprise, I discovered that I knew instinctively what I had to do or rather, not to do. So much of the challenge consisted of mastering the art of relaxation. I realised that the Impersonal power was present only when it decided to be and its simple mechanism, in this instance, was to utilise a familiar situation to give me an unfamiliar experience. I began to rock gently back and forth. I was trying to release the pressure from the unusually high concentration of energy contained inside me. A clear and intense note of music which was neither high nor low, and sounded like no instrument I had ever heard, pierced through my head like an arrow in flight, taking any stray thoughts with it. My breathing automatically deepened and I fell into a state of profound contemplation. I began to analyse the relationships I had had in my life and how I viewed them. For me, my dealings with people have, for a very long time, meant being a victim of envy, mendacity and betrayal – especially betrayal. I have read that the traditional Japanese have come to terms with the transience of life. My interpretation of their beliefs is that they consider that it is their deity's way with human beings that they are only allowed to appreciate the joys of the seasons for a certain amount of time before they are visited by death and destruction. I have always been impressed by Japanese architecture. I'm not talking about the big cities here, but the older towns and villages where the houses are constructed out of paper, with light wooden frames built in preparation for the great number of earthquakes they are subject to, so the people are not crushed by steel and concrete (as a nation they endure more earthquakes than any other in the world). My relationships with people have become like paper houses to me – or prefabs even – quick to build and even quicker to demolish. Friendships and feelings have invariably come tumbling down around me, like battered kites, the bright painted kind that flap about on the ground like dying butterflies. They are so magnificent, so elaborately decorated, so beautiful. Yet a little gust of wind and they are blown off course. I had often wondered "Is this life's great lesson – for me at least, that I will be betrayed?" I thought about my wife. She was considered nothing more than an average-looking girl by others, but they say that love is blind and when I was in love with her, she was perfect. She was only sixteen when I both met and married her. Through her, I discovered that the same mouth that passionately kisses and ardently promises, can turn around – and those very same lips will spit lies and unjust accusations against you, in favour of another, utterly devastating you in the process. Throughout my life, I had placed my trust in many things and people, hoping and praying that they would support my tenuous sanity and allow me to love and be loved. I had always been disappointed and now I know why. I had found, in unique circumstances, the co-conspirator in my life. There is certain complicity in opposites – the one serves the other. In my case, my emotional tragedy became a springboard and my pain became my hope and inspiration. You see, I've been left with neither faith in god nor man. I am on my own, but I know that the answer lies within myself. I let out a great sigh as a sudden burst of intense pleasure released itself like a tidal wave inside me, breaking through the dam of thoughts which were holding it back. It started to race unhindered through my body. I gave myself up to this extreme pleasure, although at times it became too much to bear and I begged for it to stop.

"Don't tell yourself that pleasure is unbearable, you are designed to bear it – not the pains and anguish you embrace so readily. Stop resisting – it's you that hangs on so desperately to pain, not the other way around."

For the first time in my life, I felt that I was accepting myself. If I could not be my own ally, then who would be? I realised that most of the time I walked around experiencing nothing but tension and stress. How simple, how enjoyable to abandon my questionable habits, just for a moment, and familiarise myself with the exhilarating sensation of being aware of my own life-force! I looked up at the mirror. My reflection smiled back at me with a broad spontaneous grin. Then, while I sat expressionless and still, save for my gentle rocking motion, it threw back its head and laughed a long, deep, happy exclamation. I felt no reaction as my reflection was revealed as having a life of its own. I was not frightened. I closed my eyes for a moment and drew in a deep breath. Then I realised that I was deliberately not opening my eyes for the fear of what they might see. This might seem paradoxical, but I will qualify myself by saying that, while I definitely was not afraid, a part of me was responding automatically in an attempt to spare me from anything that could possibly upset the status quo. When I realised that it was merely a reflex action I opened my eyes.

My mirror image smiled a simple smile then rose, in a single agile movement from the sitting position. It paused and looked back at me. It was waiting to see if I was paying attention, then turned around, the childlike smile not leaving the upturned lips. It began to run through and into the mirror. My eyes were firmly planted on its back as it ran onwards in a curious, slow-motion manner, like a man walking on the moon. From out of the corners of my eyes I kept glancing at either side of the now naked torso as it continued its strange exercise. At first, all I could see was my bedroom and the furniture inside it sweeping past. The same chairs, bed and curtains passed several times before “we” were “out” and running under the sky. The silent run proceeded along familiar coastal paths near my home, through grassy meadows and stony tracks and foothills under a hot midday sun. Each scene would change abruptly as if someone were swapping slides in a projector specifically designed for my benefit. I passed through countless landscapes, some familiar, some not so familiar. Although I could both see and smell, I was unable to hear a single sound save that of my own breathing and should I inadvertently “touch” anything, the initial tactile contact would disappear, as if everything was in the constant process of retreating. It reminded me of the times when I would gaze into shop windows at the objects displayed inside, my face right up close with the fingers of my open hand pressed against the glass. I was neither allowed to slow my pace down nor speed it up. I had to run at a steady pace. I am not sure about whether it was my imagination or whether it was real, but I could feel the sweat pouring down my back.

“I”, the “runner”, came across a town centre which seemed to consist of nothing but streets and avenues running straight and parallel criss-crossing each other like in Los Angeles or Manhattan. I never travelled far down any of them, just repeatedly crossed over the roads, one block at a time. I always used a set of traffic lights and always when the signs were green. I began to feel like a pawn on a chessboard. For some reason, I unexpectedly lost my concentration and looked down. When I looked up again, a tired version of myself stared back at me, dressed in my old cotton shirt and slacks. I leaned forward and reached out to touch the glass. As I trailed my hand across the mirror, I half expected the reflected images of my fingers to fall away and start doing their own thing, but nothing happened. By now everything had returned to normal. I stood up and yawned. My back was sticky with sweat. For a moment I caught myself in the mirror and jumped. My face wore the same expression as the runner. It had the same, simple upturned smile and the same glistening eyes but it was the expression on my own face. Feeling a little dreamy, I wandered off into my kitchen and drank a good deal of refrigerated mineral water.

Later on that day, shortly before 6 o'clock, I went out for a "real" run. It was something I did as often as possible but, according to my doctor, not often enough. I went to the local park which was large and well-tended and only one block away. I ran down the street, which was quite busy with people returning from work and in through the park gates. I ran once around the artificial lake and through the woods, before I began to tire. Later, in a question and answer encounter with my friend, I was told that I should take plenty of exercise, eat well and generally keep an eye on my health. He explained to me that to encounter such dynamic forces at close hand would place a great physical and emotional strain on me. On another occasion I asked what special power the mirror in my bedroom had to transform itself from a regular household effect to the "window on a world" which it was becoming.

"I have so many things to show you," came my friend's answer, "and the Impersonal world wants to open its doors up to you so that you may enter and witness the beauty of it for yourself. A mirrored surface was employed so that you could simultaneously feel close to and separate from anything you saw and felt. When you gazed at your reflection, you could be caught off guard and many secrets shown to you. If solid, three-dimensional forms had manifested in your home, you might well have become too terrified to continue. If, on the other hand, films or video recordings had been used, you would have dismissed them as unreal or fake. In your case, the mirror is a perfect medium to be used – don't ask me why, it has worked out that way due to the unique characteristics belonging to your persona. It was you who chose the mirror; it was you who chose me to come to you as a friend. What I have just said will probably not make any sense to you right now so I don't want you to waste time thinking about it. Just take it a day at a time."

Late that evening, I sat around reading or watching TV. I was feeling pretty pleased with myself. However, I was in for a nasty surprise as the malicious powers of the persona were put into play later on that night. I had a very strong feeling that I should sit and perform a few relaxation techniques before I went to bed as I had undergone a tremendous amount of exertion during the day, and had become very tense as a result. Some other "voice" convinced me that I was tired. Its rationale went along these lines:

"I had had quite a day …. I had more physical exercise than I was used to …. what I needed was some sleep."

I stood for a while looking longingly at my bed with its crisp clean linen, nice plump duvet and the neatly folded blue pyjamas sitting on the pillow. Oh, I just couldn't resist. I went over and pulled on my pyjamas, all the time unconsciously avoiding any reflective surfaces and slid into bed. The clean sheets smelt delicious reminding me of my childhood. I wriggled my toes with delight and lay spread-eagled, letting out a sigh of relief. Everything was all over, for today at least. Within minutes I had drifted off into a half sleep and I dreamt. I was drifting through unknown, unmarked and unlit alleyways. It was neither night nor day, neither dusk nor dawn. It seemed like a place which possessed no name and where time did not exist. I was following a man who could not be seen, except for his gigantic shadow which I traced along brick walls topped with broken glass and rusted corrugated iron fences. I followed him to a deserted children's playground that was lit up, not brightly, but just enough to make out a few recognisable shapes; a see-saw, slide, a climbing frame and a couple of swings, yet when I looked around to discover the source of the light, I could find none. The shadow man wandered like a lost soul, until it came across something lying on the ground which attracted its curiosity. It leaned over and peered at what seemed like a small, ragged child. The shadow man (as now I could see that it was a solid, three-dimensional creature with loose features like a human face) made curious grunting and whining sounds, as he poked and prodded the object on the floor. He began to chuckle and bent to pick up what now appeared to be an old abandoned doll. I walked over to take a closer look at what the creature held in his great paws. It was a doll, all twisted and broken with filthy rags for clothes and an animated, painted china face, with fearful eyes and a set mouth. It looked as if even hope had abandoned it.

I moved in closer, to study its features in greater detail. I fancied that it was the expression on a face that had caught a glimpse of Hell and could not forget what it had seen. My perspective changed suddenly, so that I was now looking up at a grim and shadowy visage that loomed over me like a dark cloud. A black, toothless mouth moved and a bony finger stroked my chest, in an unmistakably threatening gesture.

"You are so weak, you are so weak," it repeated mauling me, with those great damp flopping paws, which seemed as if they had to fight hard to maintain their shape, yet at the end of them were long bony appendages, like claws. I tried to wriggle free but my body was limp and powerless. There was not a part of me I could move, not even my eyes – they stared out in unblinking terror.

I awoke sitting up abruptly. My body felt stiff and one glance in the patterned mirror on the wall to the side of me confirmed that I was wearing the same expression as the doll's face had done in the dream. I sat still for a while, panting, my eyes still staring ahead, until they eventually watered over and I was forced to blink. I wiped them with the backs of my hands. I wanted to blow my nose and clear my throat. Beads of sweat covered my face and neck and the small of my back felt clammy. There were tissues beside the bed so I turned on the lamp and cleaned myself up. I had been terrified by my nightmare. I was badly shaken up, as if I had been running along quite confidently when I had suddenly crashed into a brick wall. There was a lesson to be learnt here. I should learn to discriminate between what I "felt" and "knew" I had to do, and what my personal voice was urging me to do. I should have committed myself to my exercises before crawling off to bed. The figure in my dream was right. I was still weak and extremely susceptible to making gross misjudgements, and just when I thought that I was doing so well. The creature had been genuinely frightening, mostly because it seemed to exist only as a kind of disconcertingly solid shadow, which one would normally associate with something of no substance or potency. Yet in this case, I knew that it possessed power – the power to reduce me to an impotent and frightened puppet in its hands. That absolutely horrified me. I did not know much about skilled dream interpretation, but being an analytical person, I decided that in some way, my dream monster represented the intangible "personal" powers or my "persona", the existence of which I had been made aware of by my Impersonal friend, for the first time in my life. And just as I had been warned, I had been tricked again. I looked at the clock. I had been asleep no more than 40 minutes – there was still time to put things right. It took some effort to get out of bed but I did.

I sat down on the edge of my bed. That did not feel quite right, so I moved around the room, until I found myself before the large mirror. I sat down cross legged on the floor, and began a simple breathing exercise. After a few minutes, I felt a great deal better. I wasn't used to sitting in that position and quickly became uncomfortable, so I shuffled over to the wardrobe and leant against it, with my knees tucked up. Once again I was guided into the place I had decided to describe as a "cathedral" inside my own mind.

There I felt the presence of my friend, neither speaking nor instructing me. It was just there, like a really good friend who is able to sit in silence with you. I felt great comfort in the fact that I did not need to labour to make myself understood, because my friend knew me better than I knew myself. I had accepted this "inner" friend as my guide to becoming the person I wanted to be. I felt an extraordinary depth of gratitude at having such a chance.

My body began to rock gently, swaying backwards and forwards, as it had done earlier in the evening. I felt like a delicate flower head, fixed on a slender stem, blown by the wind – the wind itself having caused the flower to evolve into its present shape, as if the movement between the two somehow gave testimony to their long established relationship. I sat for a while until the wind had died down. My body ached a little and I was very tired, but I felt at peace. The allure of abandoning myself to sleep had lost its impact – now it was merely a physical necessity. I realised it was far healthier to sort myself out before I went to sleep. After all, when I awoke wouldn't all my problems still be there, waiting for me? I went over to the bed and once again slipped underneath the duvet, spread myself out and fell asleep.

During the following weeks owing to the fact that I didn't have to work, I became excited about the fact that I could give all of my concentration to the newly discovered Impersonal side of my life. The time in-between, I would fill in a variety of ways, behaving in a more spontaneous manner, rather than laying careful plans, as was my usual habit. I had a tendency to organise my activities in order to gain whichever experience I decided upon having, grabbing at things rather than being receptive to what was on offer. I realised that I was a great deal less liberated than I had always imagined myself to be. I was also somebody who had been completely brainwashed since birth; someone who had been taken in by an endless stream of propaganda, right up until the present. I could see quite plainly that I had always been told what to do, what to expect and what to feel, all along the line. Everyone who had ever played a part in my life, had collectively, admittedly with my full permission, managed to steer me away from knowing my own self, leaving me in a state of total ignorance as to my true nature.

In the two weeks that followed, I prepared extensive notes which I would usually sit and write after any event I considered significant or memorable. I also included much of my own personal thoughts and revelations. Looking back over my notes, I saw a pattern beginning to emerge. All meetings with the Impersonal friend, and all the time spent in power situations, were doors and windows which looked in on the Impersonal world. I knew it would not be long now before I would be ready to do more than merely peer through windows and knock on closed doors.

CHAPTER SIX

The Roar from Across the River

January 18

I woke up at exactly 5.31 a.m. and almost bounced out of bed. I was beginning to notice a pattern developing in my sleeping habits. I was more active, both mentally and physically, in the early hours of the morning and the latter part of the evening. Now I would not sleep for more than six hours a night. I decided to fit the encounters into my day, in such a way as to maximise on my personal strengths and today was no exception. I knew that there was a great sense of urgency and much to be accomplished. I went into the living room as usual with a cup of coffee and a magazine, and began to idly flick through the pages, relaxation being a task I always found difficult to achieve. I needed to feel quite confident that I would be able to cope with anything that might be put against me. It was all down to trusting in the methods of the Impersonal powers. I had, from time to time, been an extremely trusting individual, but as many times as I had trusted, I had been disappointed, as I have reiterated many times. Having become accustomed to betrayal, even allied to it, had made me close up, keeping people at what I considered to be a healthy distance. I was like an oyster that would have to be prised open with a strong sharp knife to get to the soft insides. I remembered doing that when I was a teenager travelling around Europe. At one stage, I had found myself sitting on the shores of the Mediterranean, in a small fishing bay, somewhere in between the glamorous hotels of Nice and Monaco. Some friends and I had stolen a crate of oysters from some unwary fishermen and a little French kid was teaching us how to open them. First you stab the mollusc in between the valves on its shell, and then viciously twist the knife. After you get the knack, you can start to feel quite proud of yourself. Sometimes you don't even bother to eat the contents, it's just fun to do. I had never before put myself in the oyster's position, but now I was looking at it from a different point of view. If they know that one day they were going to create pearls or perhaps some of them already have, they would naturally want to protect themselves. I knew deep down that I was meant to be treasured, not consumed. It was no wonder that I had inevitably closed off and become a cynical and rather cold individual. It was merely an effort to prevent myself from suffering any further emotional damage. My thoughts were interrupted by the ringing of the telephone. I immediately felt threatened. With a great deal of suspicion, I inched my way over to it and tentatively lifted the receiver. Who was trying to disturb me so early in the morning? I looked at the DVD clock display; it read 6.16 a.m.

"You seem to be in a reflective mood this morning. You are getting to know your Impersonal self. For instance, why would the ringing of the telephone provoke such a reaction in you? You receive business calls at all hours of the day and night, even when you are on vacation. You didn't realise it, but the persona knew who was on the other end of the line."

It was my friend's voice and hearing it through the telephone receiver immediately threw me into a panic. The truth about my situation came home to me in a landslide.

I had stepped out of my safe little world of so-called normality for good. There was no turning back. My home had become a place of power and all normal rules of behaviour had been evicted. The true impact of my "surreal" encounter with my own living reflection together with a sudden acceptance of my friend as a tangible force which interfered with my perceptions at will, and also employed external mechanisms to do so, was a shock to my system. I involuntarily dropped the telephone receiver. It clanged as it fell and swung beside the table. After some time, I rather reluctantly retrieved it and held it up to my ear.

A low chuckle reverberated through my head. It seemed to emanate from both inside and outside of me at the same time. I shook my head stupidly.

"Relax! I don't know what kind of tame and manageable power you think you've been dealing with. You should have learnt by now that there is nothing to fear from me. You call me friend, after all. Things have become a little far-fetched for you to deal with, haven't they? Look, it doesn't matter, just because something is familiar doesn't mean it is going to be good for you. The opposite is also true. I will never cause you harm, and nothing that happens to you as a result of your determination to undertake this journey will harm you. Think back to your unhappy, unfulfilled, narrow-minded life. You could hardly even describe it as a "life" – it was just the faintest hope that one day you might discover what life really is. Weren't you looking for something "out of the ordinary", so that you would be able to feel special? I have told you before, I don't obey rules!"

I was slowly regaining my composure while my friend spoke. For some reason, no matter what the subject matter or the tone of voice, the effect the "Impersonal" voice had on me would always be a profoundly soothing one. I was beginning to realise that my role in this whole affair was about to change. I was now required to become more of a participant in my journey, demonstrating I had both understood that which had been communicated to me, and was also able to incorporate that understanding into my practical affairs. Whilst I was doing all this thinking, I had idly placed the receiver back down and had wandered back to my comfortable old chair. I was ashamed that I felt fear every step of the way, whenever things became a little different from how I imagined them to be. I sighed. Would I ever be relieved of my fears? When I remembered that I had just put the phone down, my mind jumped. "You've hung up! What are you doing?", but although this momentary panic caused some discomfort, I knew that my instinct to put the phone down had been correct. You can't "cut off" the lines of communication which originate from the Impersonal power any more than you can stop the tides from turning.

"You're right. You are not King Canute!

"You have created certain personal beliefs and ideologies in order to make your life easier and which have been programmed into you. But if you consider for a moment, haven't these ideas caused you nothing but confusion and discomfort? You consider your life to be a mess, with no foundation, like a house built on sand, forever crumbling away.

"At present, your emotions are still governed by fear. I know that you have recognised this and are frustrated by the fact. You must learn to accept change and not constantly and stubbornly resist the inevitable. Change is merely the process of evolution. You must also learn to accept the present situation, no matter how it is presented to you. You must go beyond your personal world to where neither fear nor failure exists. Let me explain a little of the nature of the power you are now dealing with. It can attract anything or anyone to it. Even dull, negative and malicious forces are drawn to the Impersonal ideal, when it is expressed. They are impressed by the quality they see and unsuccessfully seek to emulate that quality for their own rather dubious purposes. As you become one with this power, you will possess an attraction that will draw others to you because your whole life-style will demonstrate positivity, energy and concentration. You will become your own persona and this freedom will impress others. Everybody wants to escape tyranny. Complete this journey which you have started and you will learn what success is. I know that being successful has always been high on your list of achievements."

My reluctance to accept that my metamorphosis, although at times uncomfortable, was also miraculous, showed up my tendency to play the reluctant hero. As usual I was feeling extremely self-critical after hearing my friend's words. During each encounter, a mirror was being held up to me and sometimes I did not like what I saw.

January 22nd

I had become quite used to the "runner" who lives inside my own reflection, invested with a life of its own, who escorted me through and beyond my personal barriers into what seemed to be a place where I was able to view the limitless possibilities of the Impersonal world. I say view – because I was always on the move, not yet ready to stop and enter such a place unaccompanied. I also knew that when my time came I would have to be completely alone.

The "runner" had taken my consciousness with it into its world. A world containing so many variables all of which were transient and fleeting, and once I had left that world, my memory of any events that I had witnessed, quickly faded, in a similar way in which dreams are eventually forgotten after being so vividly recalled upon waking. Afterwards, I would always feel rejuvenated, as if I had taken some real physical exercise. Once, I was even startled to find salt in my clothes!

It was now evening and I had just finished cooking and eating a rather special dinner I made for myself (instead of the usual take-outs I had a habit of ordering on a regular basis) and, in dining alone, yet taking great care with the preparation of my food, I felt that I was in some way allowing myself a small reward. I had ceased my questioning and doubting of the Impersonal friend and was beginning to conduct myself as if I was directly answerable to it. I was confident about the validity of what I was doing, and by behaving in such a way, I saw that I was actually taking the reins of my life in my own hands for the first time.

As I sat dozing after dinner that evening, I dreamt I was hearing my friend speaking to me. In response, I asked if I were truly making progress.

"Yes, you have achieved a lot. By listening carefully to me, and by accepting what has been said, you have started to relax and stop ordering life about to suit yourself. Life has a pace of its own, and you are beginning to synchronise yourself with it. This is as a result of your time spent in the mirror technique. What you find there is not of great importance. The way you react is. The way things happen is unique to you and is, in a sense, a reflection of the real you. I, myself, have no way of really knowing what you might find there. However, I can show you how to conduct yourself. How you behave is of vital importance. There is no room for mendacity in this life. You are, in colloquial terms, having to put your money where your mouth is."

Was I mistaken or was this benevolent power becoming more relaxed with me?

"The quick answer to that is that you are the one who is starting to relax. I am the same as I have always been. You are starting to perceive me as a true friend for the first time although you have been referring to me that way in your thoughts for the sake of definition, from the beginning. I hope you can appreciate the difference. Now wake up, you need to be alert for what I have to say to you!"

I woke up and found myself squashed in my armchair with a magazine on my lap. An advertisement lay splashed across the open pages. The caption read, "Your once in a lifetime chance to realise your dreams." There was a large full colour photo of a brand new luxury home. The symbolic meaning I enjoyed attaching to such things did not escape me. It took a few moments for me to adjust to being awake. My friend was there, I could feel its presence inside me and all around where I sat. It was a pleasure to know that once again I was being kept company even when I slept. I could remember:

"You would soon know if I was not with you in some form or another. The reason you heard me while you slept was to let you know that I am able to be there for you, in all stages of consciousness. This means that you are forced to realise that you have no secret life anymore and that you are accountable to the Impersonal power at all times.

"Right now, at this point in your life, you are required to make a decision. Your personality will redouble its efforts and resort to many forms of diversions in order to prevent you from continuing on your journey. It's open season for you right now. This constant struggle is one that you can and must, eventually deal with. It is not the way of power to procrastinate. Merely by abstaining you may consider defeat automatic. It is inevitable that at some stage you have to face what is inside you. At this point in your journey things are critical. Once you have made the decision to do whatever is necessary, you will be unable to turn back. Whatever the outcome, there will be nowhere for you to retreat to once you have gone beyond this point. So I am challenging you! Are you going to give it everything you have? One thing – before you answer, you must be absolutely confident that you will be able to deal with your persona. You have the ability, of that I am certain, but you must also know it for yourself. The journey ahead can only be undertaken by someone who recognises their fears and can isolate and control them. Can you; are you able to persevere regardless of the risks? Are you ready to make such a decision? It is one that you will have to reach alone, without my intervention. I cannot help you, except to say I have absolute confidence in you. However, I cannot accept responsibility for your final decision."

My most immediate feeling was that I, in reality, had no decision to make. My direction had already been mapped out for me. I knew that not to go forward meant, I would inevitably slide backwards, and I did not want to die a slow death at the hand of my own lack of respect for myself and my life. There really was no option but to go forward. I was now convinced of the necessity to continue, despite any obstacles. I had already frittered away half my life, pursuing fruitless activities. It was now up to me to give my friend the trust deserved, and let this power start working for me.

I was heartily sick of being buffeted around, only to experience despair and disillusionment at every turn, and I considered that it was now long overdue for a chance to rebel against whatever weaknesses were still dominating me. That was it; the decision was made. I sat for a while, quite still and silent. I was being allowed time, time to understand and fully realise what to go forward really meant.

January 23rd

All day long, I was aware of a sense of urgency which surrounded my activities. I could not escape the feeling that all the events in my life had been endured or enjoyed as preparation for what was about to begin. I was not afraid. Soon, I would be giving my greatest performance and at this very moment I was waiting in the wings. I was aware of the presence of power all throughout my day, yet it was a feeling which I was able to feel comfortable with, like first night nerves before walking out onto a stage to act out my part in a play. My friend had hinted at the nature of my next encounter, so I decided that the wisest thing to do was to prepare myself accordingly; to gather all my strength and to adjust myself to the fact that anything might happen. I waited all day to receive a clue from my friend, but I was left alone completely until the evening of the 24th.

January 24th

It was shortly before sunset when I entered into an encounter. I had amassed a great deal of curiosity over the last 48 hours. The information I required was given to me and concerned many practical preparations. This is what was said:

"You have made your decision. The door which was opened for you has now been closed forever. You are now a subject of the Impersonal realm. All its power will be made available to you. If in a moment of weakness, you might allow yourself to slide, you would without doubt be ambushed by your persona, which has lost you to the Impersonal and is anxious to regain control. As I am constantly repeating, be aware of this at all times, but do not allow the possibility of an attack intimidate you. You have come too far to suffer a defeat now. You must have absolute belief in yourself and completely disregard the way you used to behave. Trust each situation that you are faced with, although the reason for it might not be apparent at the time. Be resolute!"

"I am now going to give you the following instructions, which you must carry out to the letter. You need to get away from your home. Find somewhere to stay for the next two weeks. You must choose a place that is part of the unspoilt wilderness, as far away from the city as is reasonably possible. Make sure that you are surrounded by both woodlands and water; water is especially important. It must be present as a dominating feature, like a waterfall or a river. It must also be possible for you to be left undisturbed. A peaceful environment is essential."

Almost immediately, Big Bear Mountain, a tranquil resort located within one of the National Reserves, sprang to mind. It fitted all requirements splendidly, with its comfortable and modern cabins to rent. However, I could not help but shudder when I pictured the great lake at Big Bear. It must be at least 200 feet deep, with treacherous, slippery vines which grew up and out from the lake side and floated to the surface. For a moment, my mind went blank as if a giant brake had been applied. I was terrified of water, even though I lived close to the ocean. I had never learnt to swim. I tried hard to think of somewhere else I could go, but all the time my mind would return to Big Bear knowing instinctively that it was the right place and that I would not be able to avoid whatever it was that I was destined to encounter there. Earlier I had considered myself prepared for anything – but not for this. I broke out into a cold sweat, so great was my fear. I was about to surrender to another one of my panic attacks, when (and it is difficult for me to describe the sensation exactly) something inside me sort of switched itself on. An as-yet undiscovered and unnamed part of me had activated itself automatically, in a direct response to my terror. I was annoyed that I was sitting there in such a state and about nothing. I went over to the living room windows and swung them wide open. It was a cool night with a refreshing breeze blowing in from the Pacific. I stood there for a while watching the sunset, which seemed particularly magnificent this evening. The sun was a great, heavy golden ball that was gradually sinking into the ocean, as if its weight were too much for the sky to bear. Its descent was marked by a blood red curtain which drew across the sky contrasting patriotically with a deep royal blue, the first colour to indicate nightfall. My imagination which had seemed so engulfing when I experienced it, was gradually cut down to manageable proportions.

This was a good sign. I was learning to bring myself under more and more control, each time something like this happened. I wondered why, after being my closest ally for all of my life, my own personality or persona, should turn out to be so self-destructive. I needed an answer.

"You are right, your persona has done nothing but try to protect you. But, it has become over protective, dominant and bombastic. You have been so afraid to live your life that you almost decided to stop living altogether. I have said that change is evolution and now it is time to make some changes. If you like, your persona got you this far, but it is unable to take you any further. It really is very simple. Life is offering you a way to bring about a change of attitude. You are at a particularly vulnerable age too, when many people like to settle down into their chosen life-style having decided that they don't want to change, to learn or to grow. They can become stubborn, set in their thoughts and have rigid ideas. Be active; be prepared to change your mind; be willing to learn. This whole process you are going through is set up the way it is in order to benefit you and for no other reason. Above all, relax and enjoy yourself. You are quite a hard person and you are certainly too hard on yourself for your own good. Now continue with your preparations."

The remainder of the day was spent making the necessary arrangements, like making a reservation for the cabin. Of course there was a vacant cabin, the only one free for the exact time that I would need it. "That was no coincidence," I thought to myself as I put the phone down. I considered myself the subject of a conspiracy, conducted by an autocratic yet benevolent power, with which I was beginning to feel quite at home. I picked out a good sized suitcase and filled it with enough clothes to last at least twelve days. Looking at my selection of city casuals and designer suits, I thought ruefully, "I'll be more likely to need a suit of armour." I reflected on my life-style. It was far from ideal. Okay, it looked good from everybody else's point of view, but what good was that to me? Fancy apartment, a fancy car (I was the proud owner of a brand new Jaguar XJS, as well as a Cherokee and a regular old station wagon). Attractive, yet strictly casual girlfriends would visit my apartment (although at the time when I encountered the Impersonal friend I'd been single for some time) – but, and this was the big question – did it impress me? All those things were nice (especially the English car; I'm a bit of an enthusiast) yet they failed absolutely to allow me to feel fulfilled. I would have happily traded the whole lot for that feeling, but so far my friend had not indicated the necessity to become a bag man. I was relieved to know that living well was not an obstacle to happiness.

I brought the cooler box in from the garage and also packed a supply of tinned food. There was no real need to worry about suppliers. There was a supermarket as well as other stores at the resort including a diner, which, if I remember correctly, sold the best doughnuts I'd ever tasted. I mention this because I had begun to notice that since my first encounter with my friend, I had developed an uncharacteristic craving for sweet food. I usually never went further than the occasional ripe banana, but just lately I'd started adding at least two spoonfuls of sugar to my tea and often three or four when drinking coffee. My fridge, too, was never without candy and one particular brand of ice cream. Sometimes, I'd do things like miss out on a meal and consume an entire family-size chocolate cake! I began to load up the station wagon and check that the snow chains were in the emergency kit. They would be indispensable should it snow at Big Bear, as it sometimes did at this time of year, although not often.

About two hours later, everything was in order. All that was left for me to do was to lock up my apartment, leave a note for the dairy man and ask my neighbour to check my mailbox from time to time. With everything settled, I climbed into the driver's seat. As I adjusted the rear-view mirror, I caught a glimpse of my reflection; my eyes were clear and untroubled. I put the key into the ignition and the engine roared to life. As I drove away I thought of a quotation from G. K. Chesterton. It went "An able man shows his spirit by gentle words and resolute actions; he is neither hot nor timid."

I had been driving for approximately ninety minutes when, upon glancing in the rear-view mirror, I was suddenly thrown into confusion at the sight of a man sitting in the back seat. The near paralysing shock made me momentarily lose concentration, resulting in the car almost going out of control. I looked behind me – the back seat was empty. I checked the rear-view mirror again. There was my "passenger", sitting stone faced, his eyes looking forward in an unblinking stare. I put my foot down on the accelerator, which was ridiculous if you think about it, but the last thing I was doing was behaving in a rational manner. My breathing became short and erratic. This was unbearable. It was all the more disconcerting knowing that I could only see my passenger in the mirror. I desperately needed to understand the significance of such a bizarre manifestation and whether or not it meant to do me harm. Of course, I assumed that its only purpose would be a malevolent one. Flashes of neon lit up the interior of the car but not the man's face. He looked almost featureless, so blank was his stare. I was perched on the edge of my seat and drove uncomfortably this way for several miles, half expecting to either be throttled from behind or to crash the car. Eventually the time came, that when I looked into the rear-view mirror, my unwelcome passenger had left. I slowed down and pulled over at the first opportunity. I was aware of a very strong instinct in me. It was that of survival, which had been activated in order to ensure that I wouldn't meet my death in an auto crash, like the poor devil I had witnessed not so long ago. I was absolutely terrified, clambered out of my seat, opened the car door and leant heavily across it.

A little later, I was to be found standing by the roadside, drinking in the evening air. I had turned off the freeway and was now on a mountain road. To my right was a sheer drop. What if I had lost control of the car and had plunged over the ravine's edge? How was I expected to behave normally when such things were happening right out of the blue? An explanation was due. I raged silently. Eventually, I calmed down. Everywhere I went I had to accept that there was power in my life. I realised that there was bound to be some form of "leakage" from my formal encounters when it would be least expected and that I should be prepared for such events. The more I stood thinking about it, it slowly dawned on me that my passenger had been my own reflection – not my normal one, but the one that I lived in the mirror and escorted me when I performed my reflection exercise. That's why I couldn't see it when I turned round, only in the mirror. Perhaps it was intended to be an escort, it certainly did me no harm. My imagination, on the other hand, was something to be reckoned with. Who knows what desperate acts a man could be provoked into performing, should he start to think irrationally. I found myself remembering an acquaintance of mine who had shot himself in the head about a year ago, seemingly for no apparent reason. Oh, he'd had his share of problems, but nothing that, with a little help, he would not have been able to deal with. That, I guess, was a good example. A man can drive himself to complete despair. I decided that I was being made aware of my sense of survival, of my will to live and that when it came to the crunch, I would find hidden strengths. I was required to believe in myself at all times, not just when I was expecting a trial of power. If I had strayed into my encounter with the "Impersonal" powers at first, now I was walking right into a situation fully aware that I was going to be tested. It occurred to me that, although I'd had a taste of freedom, I most certainly had not mastered it. I turned around and climbed back into my car.

The approach to Big Bear Mountain was an incredible sight. The twisting road which lead up to the resort offered splendid views of majestic, snow-capped mountains and soaring evergreens, some of which – those nearest the peaks – were still coated with layers of clean white snow. Lower down, the trees seemed denser, and more comforting. I gained further reassurance listening to the weather forecast. For the next seven days at least, clear skies and plenty of sunshine were pretty much guaranteed. I pulled over to the Information Office window and was greeted by a burly forest ranger. After a short exchange, he handed me a map of Big Bear and pointed me in the general direction of my cabin and the lodge where I had to register and pick up the key to my temporary shelter. Looking around, the resort seemed pretty deserted which suited me fine.

I had no difficulty in finding my own cabin, number 12A. It was set in a clutch of other cabins, all carrying odd numbers which were arranged on the south side of the lake (obviously 12A represented number 13, therefore catering for the more superstitious visitor). According to the map, the even numbers were somewhere lower down the mountainside, over toward the Western Gate.

It was a rustic-looking affair on the outside resembling something out of a Davy Crockett legend, whereas inside it possessed all the mod cons that you would expect to find in a purpose-built bungalow out in the suburbs. It consisted of a large bedroom, bathroom, living room and small kitchen. It was comfortable and reasonably well decorated. There would be no challenge living here, I thought.

CHAPTER SEVEN

The Impersonal World

January 25th

I have lived in cities ever since I can remember and I received a real shock at waking up to such stillness that I became agitated. Back in my city apartment I would be greeted by the sound of traffic roaring along a four-lane highway, just one block away from my residence. I would never have guessed it, but over the years it had become comforting. I looked across at the fireplace where the artificial log fire filled the room with a warm crimson glow. The windows were blue-black. It was still dark out there among the trees. Inside, in the warm, I lay rolled up in my quilt like a hot dog wrapped in a bun. I wanted a day off, to be honest – from everything. I was so happy to be alone and at peace with myself for the first time in ages, that even an "encounter" with the Impersonal friend might seem like an intrusion on what was beginning to feel like paradise; I hoped I would be understood. It was great not having to get up and start running around like a speeded up cartoon worrying about getting to work on time. Even though I'd been on vacation for several days now, I hadn't quite managed to forget my job completely. Every time I imagined opening the wardrobe back home only to face that rack of conservative ties and those black lace-up shoes, I knew my holiday would eventually come to an end and there they'd be, waiting patiently for me to jump back on the treadmill.

I had really begun to appreciate the non-committal atmosphere of early morning, before the day began and all that I could expect was the unexpected. My face was buried in my pillow when the dawn chorus began to herald in the new day. I had never heard it as I was hearing it now. Every forest and woodland bird was participating, from the throaty rumbles of the warblers to the rhapsodic trilling of the song birds and the majestic cries of the predators hovering high up in the mountains; the little ground birds proudly piped and wailed as they too proclaimed their territorial rights. What managed to capture my attention more than any other member of the fully orchestrated and divinely conducted, original "one day only" performance, was the solo. Almost directly outside of my cabin was a pair of nesting song birds. The male was a splendid artist – the Pavarotti among his fellow songsters. He arrested my attention for as long as he sang. The song was similar to that of the trilling and cheeping of the specially bred English canaries. The whole event was overwhelming – it was almost too much to bear.

The miracles did not stop there, for as I stood in the kitchen with my own special coffee percolator brought from home, mixing a favourite blend of Jamaican coffee, I could not help but find myself staring out at the high mountains whose sugar-white caps were just becoming visible as the night mists were gradually clearing. Directly in front of me was a view of a distant twin-peaked mountain that reminded me of Everest which I had seen several times in my travels. Just to complement the splendour of that which I was so privileged to witness, I took one of my favourite recordings, a selection of arias performed by Sutherland

and loaded them in to my large portable stereo. I perched on the kitchen stool hugging my knees to my chest, listening to such ecstatic offerings as the Willow Song, "O beau pays de la Touraine", and Delibes' "Bell Song" from *Lakmé*, whilst simultaneously gazing out of the window at the mountain scenery. This lit up before my eyes as the sun sneaked up from behind a line of trees belonging to the vast Sequoia Forest, which shrouded and protected Big Bear Mountain.

When I had eventually dropped down from the stool after the music had reached its last great finale, it was fast approaching midday. I was pleasantly warm and I spent a lot of time sitting outside my cabin door lazing in the sun and taking long walks through the woods. This place was thoroughly beautiful. Certain qualities that had remained buried deep inside me for years were beginning to surface. I was responding to the child in me. When I was young, before our family moved to England, my parents would always take me out to explore the wilderness of the great parks. I remember being happy and carefree back then and an echo of that simple feeling was returning, inspired by my surroundings. I decided that to have the qualities of a child reawakened in me would only work to my advantage. What better qualifications could I have than resilience, strength and honesty? I would fight with the fearlessness of a child; it would do nothing but benefit me in the power struggle that I anticipated would lie ahead of me. I was beginning to see the strategy behind the need for me to be here. It was also unfamiliar to my persona, thereby reducing the strength of its grip on me.

It was early afternoon and I was sitting on a log in a clearing with my face turned slightly toward the sun. Almost imperceptibly, with a studied gentleness, I was joined by my friend. For a while we were like two best friends sitting together in the silence, as only people who are really close to each other know. After quite some time a dialogue began.

"How do you like your new environment? You will discover the importance of this move as the days go by, but for the time being, you are correct in thinking that it is at least an advantage just to be in unfamiliar surroundings, wherever they may be. It is very difficult for you to deny the existence of all that you have previously identified with. Up until now all that you have had to turn to for help is you own cunning and resourcefulness, but the Impersonal powers that have already taken root within you are now ready and able to respond to your needs. An important clue is not to 'try' too hard. There is no 'trying' only 'being' and 'doing'. The world is full of triers! Instead of labouring away with your own clumsy efforts to combat your fears, let go and allow the Impersonal side of your nature to accomplish your goals for you. In allowing it free rein you will find yourself performing in a way that will surprise you. You have so much to learn about yourself. I can only keep repeating, your persona, as you have witnessed, is extremely subtle. It will even seek your sympathy in an attempt to make you feel sorry for it; but in the same way that your persona knows your darkest fears, so the 'Impersonal' power knows your greatest strengths, therefore in a moment you can change your position from that of extreme disadvantage, to that of invincibility. There is nowhere for you to run and nowhere to hide because everywhere you go, you take yourself with you. Have you ever thought of it like that? And it is you who harbours irrational thoughts and retains the potential to harm yourself, no one else! Now is the time to confront them squarely and gain complete control, and you must do it alone. If you succeed, the powers of your persona will automatically turn and serve you. You will lose both your dreams and your nightmares!

"Tonight, you must do exactly as I tell you. You must wait until after dark, go to the top of the ridge which overlooks the lake, sit and wait. What you will be doing is creating a set-up which will bring your fears out into the open. It is necessary for you to be face to face with your terror otherwise it will remain wilful and elusive and you will never achieve mastery over it. When you do this, have absolute confidence, if not in yourself, then in the 'Impersonal' powers which will be working for you."

It seemed strange somehow to discover that my persona, which had become so familiar to me, had now been identified as my mortal enemy. For so long it had been my "best friend". I had imagined myself to be indivisible from it until I encountered another part of myself which had alerted me to the fact that I was keeping bad company. I remembered a story of a famous Hollywood actor who had literally hired a bodyguard to protect himself from himself. It was an interesting notion, I thought, and an extremely imaginative and humorous approach to that particular individual's dilemma. Sadly, it hadn't worked and he had died from a drug overdose.

I was an impatient person who possessed a nagging obsession with having the future stamped and guaranteed for me. More than ever I wanted my friend to reassure me about the outcome of this power-play, but I knew that it was a futile wish. Of course my power lay in my ability to act, not to sit and daydream, so I rose and walked back to my cabin.

Later in the evening, after a little sleep and a good deal of slumming, I made preparations for the night's vigil. I filled my thermos with some English tea (it affected my nerves less than coffee which I drank far too much of anyway) and rolled up my down-filled sleeping bag so that I would have something comfortable to sit on. I decided not to take any food with me although I had a sneaking feeling that I might regret the decision. I was dressed in warm clothes as the nights could be chilly at this time of year. There was a flashlight in my canvas bag just in case the sky clouded over. I stood for a while at my cabin door looking out at the shadowy forest. I felt like a soldier about to march on the enemy. It was with great determination that I turned and locked the door behind me. It was a simple and routine action, yet also symbolic, as I left the safety of the cabin and walked out into the night. There was a fist in my stomach, as my nerves wound themselves up in preparation for what I could not resist in imagining as a melodramatic encounter with strange and unknown forces. It had to be something dramatic I felt sure, a chance to test my powers! I could see the ridge from where I was standing. It was about three hundred yards away. Fifteen minutes later and I reached the exact spot which my friend had pointed out. I spread the sleeping bag out on the rocky surface and sat down. I looked up at the constellations and tried to recognise the few with which I was familiar. I loved their names. I recognised the Plough or Big Dipper, also Cassiopeia, the great W or M depending on which way you view it, and the twin stars Castor and Pollux. I was also able to distinguish the Pleiades, the Seven Sisters huddled together, feint yet unmistakable. I slowly began to trace the constellation of Orion, the Hunter, with his belt of three stars and the shape of his drawn bow marked by the large star on the left. It fascinated me how astronomers had taken a random display of stars and divided them up into recognisable groups and also why various mythical figures or alternatively, simple objects or animals were chosen to represent them: like the Plough, or Libra the Scales: take Capricorn the Goat; Ursa Major the Great Bear; Virgo the Maiden or Leo the Dragon. I have seen the Crab Nebula through a telescope, a cloud of gases crammed with enough mysteries to occupy the astronomer for a very long time. Consider how the planets have been named: Mars, god of war; Neptune, god of the oceans; Venus, goddess of love; and Mercury, winged messenger of the gods. The largest planet in our solar system was named after the definition of the 'supreme being' by the Aryan tribes of Greece, "Father Zeus, the king and father of all gods and men." It was the name, Jupiter, preferred by the Roman tribes, which eventually became the official title of that giant gaseous member of the satellites of the star, Sol. When we see what has been "brought into being" around us, we become quite desperate in wanting to fully comprehend it, thinking that it might possibly hold some clues to our group identity as inhabitants of a planet which we did not create, and with a creator whom we seem to have some difficulty coming to terms with. There is something in all of us that simply wants to find something that will make sense of everything else and we have a tendency to seek outside of ourselves for the answer. It was at this moment that I felt grateful in knowing that what I needed lay within inside me.

The evening was intensely beautiful. In great contrast to the grandeur of the constellations, the moon hung in the sky like a friendly neighbour. It shone on the surface of the lake and lit the surrounding area with a pearly light. There was total quiet, except for the occasional rustle in the undergrowth; probably a small animal foraging for food in the safety of the night. I sat for some time thinking about my life and the radical changes I had undergone in such a short time. I felt as though I had been afraid of life and had attempted to hide from its challenges. I thought of a saying. It went:

"Life loves those who dare to live it."

Throughout the years I had devoted my time to making myself comfortable and making it easy to avoid any unnecessary complications. I was like an animal curled up in its burrow which is disturbed and chased out into the open. That was the role my friend was acting out, of shaking the dust off of me and forcing me to confront my fears, a task which I would have happily avoided to the end of my days.

The quiet dignity of my surroundings continued making an impression upon me. The branches of mighty sequoia trees which stood all around, seemed to be brushing the clouds. I turned and scanned the first line of trees which shot up out of the ground, their tall symmetrical shapes defining them as solemn, silent sentinels. Between them and the indescribable beauty of the night sky, I was overcome with feelings of wonder. I leant over and took my thermos out of the bag. I sat for a while sipping my tea to ward off the chill. I regretted not bringing along some food. It would have given me something to do as well as filling my stomach. A noise like the snapping of twigs just behind me, interrupted my thoughts. I sat bolt upright. A chill ran the length of my spine and I shuddered. It felt as though my neck had been frozen over. I swung round, but whatever had made the sound was not visible. There were more noises to follow, steadily gaining in volume. My imagination began to run riot. My head was full of the most incredible scenes – mostly frightening ones involving a violent assault upon my person. The source of the noise was very close now, but despite straining my eyes, I could not distinguish what it was. I hunted frantically for my adversary in the dark shadows amongst the trees which were acting as a catalyst to my growing uneasiness. I allowed myself a grunt and a half smile. If something terrifying or alien had leapt out of the bushes, my mind, if it could, would be the first to detach itself from my brain and make like the roadrunner. I could distinguish the sound of rasping breath, which by now was so close, that I could feel its coldness on the back of my neck. The power of my imagination was far beyond anything I had ever considered. It was able to conjure up a situation fraught with fear, needing no evidence whatsoever and as a result, have me trembling from head to toe. I vainly fought to bring myself under control. It was then that I remembered my flashlight and reached over for it. I turned it on and swung round. A small deer no bigger than a lamb, stood petrified in the beam of light. After a few moments, it shook itself, turned and ran off into the bushes. It was more alarmed than I was. I let the flashlight drop onto the floor. Feeling incredibly foolish and shaking from head to foot, I sat back and went over the last five minutes in my mind. I was amazed at the way I had reacted. All the time it had only been a harmless animal wandering in the bushes. Never before had I been so aware of how extensively I allowed my imagination to rule my life. A part of me with so much potential was being exploited in an attempt to drive me insane. I finished my tea, which helped to calm my over-worked nervous system, before finding myself lying back onto the sleeping bag reflecting on what I personally considered to be the human dilemma. The only talents, I thought, that human beings seem to have perfected are those of hate, fear, greed and the ability to kill each other and the wildlife around them. Yet they still lacked the power to know themselves. It seemed to me that the persona would allow people to be anything they desired, except the one thing that would enable them to relax and be happy. I began to shake my head from side to side. Man has explored the earth from the ocean depths to the peaks of the mountains, and has even managed to travel to "that moon up there," but has hardly begun to scratch the surface of his inner nature. It seemed to me that society was perverse and irredeemable. The entire fabric of existence was rotten to the core. I became overwhelmed by a feeling of hopelessness. Everything had gone too far and was now irretrievable. Mankind is racing across the river of materialism and burning his boats behind him. "Don't people realise that they are collectively guilty of matricide?" The Impersonal friend seemed to talk a lot about "things brought into being", but what was it doing to preserve them? (It did not occur to me at that point, as I was becoming quite hysterical, that perhaps it was the duty of mankind to become the good housekeeper.) Half sitting, I picked up my thermos and hurled it at a tree. It crashed noisily into low branches rupturing the stillness of the night and causing the birds which roosted there to take flight. I sat down with a loud sigh, overcome by frustration. I looked over the side of the ridge and as I did so I was disturbed by a succession of irrational thoughts that were not my own. "If you should fall over the edge of this ravine you would be smashed into pieces. Why don't you jump? The Impersonal friend is so powerful that it would save you. Go on jump! It's safe. You're so powerful now, you won't be hurt."

Inside my head was an absolute screaming maniac. I found myself laughing nervously in an attempt to reduce the pressure from this onslaught. I was tired by now and just wanted to curl up and go to sleep. I looked longingly at my sleeping bag but decided that I couldn't possibly sleep out there. For one thing it was getting too cold for comfort and anyway, my cabin was only a short walk away. This encounter although embarrassing to me had also proved useful, because a certain element of my character had been revealed to me. This had allowed me some insight into the methods of the attack from the persona. It was a little like guerrilla warfare. The more I knew about the way it operated, the more I would be able to defend myself. I became optimistic. I was getting this whole game into the right perspective at last. Tonight was necessary, but I knew that, but the real work was yet to come. I reached my cabin and was welcomed by the warmth from the gas fire. With a grateful moan, I hugged up to it and stayed there until I was comfortable. I had disciplined myself to the point that, come what may, I would always take notes immediately after an encounter. From now on, I would include as much detail as possible, such as dates and places, the dialogue and especially the mood of the Impersonal friend. Of course I would include "power trials" such as I had undergone tonight. If I was too tired, and tonight was a good example, I would sometimes leave it until morning, but as exhausted as I was, I took up a pen and sat up for a while chronicling the events of the evening. For some unknown reason, I felt that this both peculiar and comic incident was too important to leave until a later time. I had to attend to it now while it was still fresh in my mind. I found myself laughing at the way I had behaved. I'm glad there were no witnesses to my spectacle. Eventually, I became too tired to think, so I curled up on the floor and fell asleep.

January 28th

During the last two days, I had received careful and detailed instructions to wait until late this evening, take a small boat (which I had hired that afternoon) and row out into the middle of the lake. I was given no more information about what to do or what to expect. So at the appointed hour, I went down to the water's edge, climbed into the rowing boat, pushed off from the bank and took it out to the deep water right into the centre of the lake. Again I sat waiting, bobbing about like a decoy duck set up for the hunt. Nevertheless, it seemed as if I had exhausted my capacity for being afraid the other night, for I was quite calm despite my phobia of water. I found myself marvelling at this newfound fearlessness. I definitely was not the same confused and muddled character who had taken fright the other evening and with so little cause.

I had spent the day walking in the forest, exploring the hills and had discovered that this wild and unspoilt environment surrounding me was helping to create the new man who was growing and developing every day. It contrasted vividly with the cringing 'yes' man, who would normally be found rushing around the hot and dirty city, flapping about in my designer suits, having elaborate meals in restaurants at the top of tall buildings and constantly kow-towing to the one man who held the key to my fortune, and therefore my future in his fat, smooth, perfectly manicured paws. (I had decided that it *was* his hands that had seemed to hold my future and not, as I now know, my own. Perhaps my reason for referring to my partner's hands as "paws" was the fact that they reminded me of the creature in my dream, whose power over me at that time, seemed absolute.) Once again, I began to seriously consider trading in my city life, moving up the coast and settling in one of the canyons. Sure, it wasn't exactly the wilderness, but it was a step in the right direction.

I looked up and once again traced fragments of the constellations as they showed between the great masses of cloud formations which were moving across the sky in great clumps, alternately obscuring then unmasking the moon like a form of heavenly fan dance.

There was a thunderstorm due – I could see flashes of light arcing ahead of me, travelling across the valley. From such a distance the electrical storm looked magnificent, with streaks of lightning splitting the distant blue-black sky to reveal flashes of the crimson, blue and white light hiding behind the endless bank of clouds. I held a sneaking suspicion that the secret of what I was waiting for would arrive tucked under its flanks.

The clouds which hung heavily over the lake were breaking up and drifting away, to reveal the moon's placid face. Once again its cool light hit the water only to be broken up by the swell of the waves. A little way off to my right, a low dense mist was beginning to gather just above the water's surface. I was starting to recognise a set up. There were elements around me which were intent on destroying an unwanted part of me which I, through my own repeated efforts, had so desperately tried to shake off. I shuddered at the thought of the strength and resolute nature of the power which was concentrating on me. The patch of mist which, because I had adjusted the position of my boat slightly, was now just over my right shoulder, was moving closer. I picked up the oars and adjusted my position so that I was facing a grey-green sludge which sat on the water like an oil slick. I knew it was no fluke of nature, rather some evil ominous thing which was heading deliberately towards me. It travelled quickly and soundlessly, almost like a hovercraft, until it lay within a few feet of the boat. It had an animalistic quality to it, a sort of disconcerting aliveness. It possessed the kind of tension that you would only associate with something sentient. It remained poised like a creature about to spring into action, before it began circling the boat in a way reminiscent of the methods employed by actors in the modern theatre when intimidating the "guilty" party. The accused is usually placed on a chair where his movements are restricted whilst the inquisitors continuously walk in circles around him. I kept turning my head from left to right and adopting various defence postures, whilst simultaneously ensuring that the little craft remained upright. I didn't want to be tricked into losing my balance and ending up in the water. I thought that perhaps there was something more tangible at the heart of the swirl which was about to reveal itself, when suddenly it lunged forward, enveloping me in an instant. Thick, grey tongues of some solid yet viscous substance which was foul-smelling and most unpleasant lashed around the bottom of the boat. I felt something cold and wet "licking" my skin. I called out: "Who's there, who's hiding? Why don't you come out and face me?"

I looked around. I could see nothing. All signs of the lake and shore were blotted out. The mist was thick above my head, as if I was being smothered by a layer of blankets. I tried to work out what the stuff was. It looked like mercury at first, yet it was far too animated and the foul smelling odour was not unlike human excreta. It was sticking to my hands, face and any other part of my skin which remained uncovered. It even began to seep underneath my clothing until I could feel it sticking to my neck, stomach and the back of my thighs. I was almost reduced to crying and shrieking as I desperately tried to push the stuff out from the bottom of my trousers. It was driving me crazy! I must have looked like a man who was catching on fire or someone doing an Indian war dance. The stench was so overpowering that I found myself choking and spluttering. It revolted me to such an intense degree, I was going to vomit at any minute. Eventually I found myself leaning over the side of the boat, retching violently.

From somewhere out in the water, I heard a voice calling out for help. I leaned over the side of the boat and listened in the general direction of where the sound was coming from. All the time I felt convinced that I was being tricked. Although I was not totally unconcerned my guard was up. There had been no sign of anyone in the water before I had been surrounded by the living fog.

"Help me, I'm drowning. Please, somebody help me! Please help. I can't swim."

I felt as though I had been hit with a brick, when I recognised that the voice was my own and quite simply, I lost my nerve. I slumped down to the bottom of the boat wrapping my arms around me. I began to rock slowly back and forth in an attempt to comfort myself, mindlessly humming one of my favourite tunes. I sat like this with my eyes half closed, hoping that everything would just go away and that, when I would open them again, I'd find myself back home in my city apartment, watching the TV or something. After a while, I began to feel a little better, partly due to the heat. Perhaps I was back in my centrally heated flat after all?

The heat lessened in intensity (it seemed as if it had been reaching boiling point all around me). I looked up and watched the filth that had covered me sublimate into the grey mist that had first appeared on the lake. It gathered up its skirts and fled rapidly across the water, evaporating into nothingness before it reached the shore. I cursed my weakness. I had been in control and was about to come face to face with the situation, when I had lost heart. I realised, rather ruefully, that there were still many loopholes in my defence. I rowed back to the water's edge feeling sad and dejected. I thought about going back and attempting to continue where I had left off, but I knew that it would be useless to try.

I tied the boat up at the jetty and started to trudge wearily back to my cabin.

That night, I had a dream which helped me to understand my relationship with the Impersonal power and also ridded me of my despondency at my assumed failure out on the lake. I was running down a long dark tunnel. The faster I ran, the longer the tunnel became, yet I wasn't able to slow down because something was chasing me. I could hear its laboured breathing directly behind me. Every time I slowed my pace a pair of unseen hands would snatch at my ankles. I was powerless and weak. My legs were like jelly and felt as if they might give way at any time. There was even an element in me that actually wanted to give in – after all I was going nowhere! Then I suddenly stumbled and fell to the ground. Two things happened: firstly, what felt like strong bony claws got a grip on my ankles and began to tug at me. Secondly, to my surprise, the floor vanished beneath me, so instead of falling flat on my face as you'd expect, I stopped and started to spin round in a horizontal position, just like a power drill. When I had gained enough momentum, I flipped vertically upwards and around, twisting my ankles free in the process. I turned to find myself standing upright gazing into a pair of cold, leathery, almost reptilian eyes which stared up at me from out of the darkness. I felt about ten feet tall as I peered down to take a closer look at what I thought was an animal crouched before me. I stared into its lifeless eyes for what seemed to be an eternity half expecting them to register some kind of emotion, but they remained dead and lifeless. All of my personal fears disappeared as a monumental surge of energy swept through me like a great tidal wave. It was the same sensation that I felt when I participated in my encounters, although intensified to a greater degree. I immediately identified it as a power I could control as naturally as any one of my faculties, such as my muscular strength or the power of reason. It felt surprisingly familiar. It was like standing within a citadel, an unassailable fortress of power. This was no dream; this was real. Maybe I might never feel it again, but I could no longer doubt its existence. I gazed intently at what I now recognised was my foe with a burning desire to see for myself the true form this creature took, whose eyes stared at me with unblinking calm. Almost immediately, the tunnel was filled with a stream of light which revealed the shape of my adversary. A small man stood opposite me – wearing my face! I was looking at a distorted mirror image of myself. Before I could get a good look, the "reflection" began to fold in on itself, like a newspaper in the hands of a magician, until it no longer existed. The tunnel had also disappeared and there before me lay what I recognised as the entrance to a new world; a multi-dimensional blank canvas. Everywhere, I focused my attention there was no clue, no colour, no feeling, no sound and no definition.

I awoke, knowing that I had no need to fear my own creation (for it was obvious that this creature was a caricature of my persona) and I now possessed the evidence I needed of the immense resource of power which lay inside me.

January 30th

My friend had communicated to me about both my encounter on the lake as well as my dream.

"I am pleased that you were able to recognise the fact that you did not fail when you met with the mist out on the lake. Although you didn't realise it you performed well. The crucial time was deep in the night while you slept. At that time, although you were completely unaware of the fact, the electric storm was raging all around you. During those hours, you were brought vision and insight. Although you did well on your own, there is always room for accepting help from any benevolent power which might be observing your efforts and wishes you well. You were surprised when you realised that you had not been defeated by the attack from the centre of the mist. The reason why you succeeded was because when you believed that someone might be in trouble out on the lake, you immediately recognised your own voice. That was one of the flaws in the strategy employed by your persona. It was seeking your sympathy, but it failed. In a metaphorical sense the persona itself is drowning. It is losing its hold over you. Although the true meaning of the event was lost to you at the time, you interpreted it correctly in your dream. While you were asleep you were relaxed and, as a result, you unconsciously turned and used the Impersonal power in order to deal with your fears. You must learn to act this way deliberately and consciously in your normal waking state. That is the art you must learn to master. It is the reason for your presence in this place. Now everything that you have understood should be put into practice. I have some instructions for you which you must follow carefully. You must obtain two large mirrors, and stand them vertically in such a way that they will be facing each other no more or less than six feet apart. One mirror should face East, the other directly facing West. Sit on the floor in between the two mirrors, in front of the one that faces East.

Just sit calmly as if you were about to perform your reflection exercise. You'll need to summon up all your courage in order to deal with whatever happens next, and before you ask I have no clues as to what that might be. It is between you and the representative of your persona. You deserve some credit to even consider taking on such a challenge. It takes a brave and ambitious man to enter this arena in an attempt to win back his own life. But you must follow the rules to the letter. In the Impersonal world there are no compromises. Now listen to me carefully. Immediately afterwards you must dismantle the two mirrors. Take them away from each other and smash the glass. Do it, and do it quickly – if you should hesitate – if you should delay for a second there's a chance that …."

It became difficult to hear anymore, as if the voice were addressing itself. I strained to hear.

"It only takes one sliver of broken glass, one tiny splinter is responsible for more than his own life … this world, the balance …."

My friend's voice became inaudible until there was an eventual silence. This continued for some time. I felt great respect and simply waited for the voice to continue. I was then addressed with all the authority that my friend possesses.

"You will leave room for trouble – so much trouble … just the tiniest scratch is enough. What I'm saying might seem mysterious, but you must obey my instructions implicitly. If you do not, you will cause yourself a possible lifetime of unimaginable distress. Do this thing; do it right and you will become a new man. Do not attempt this exercise until your inner voice tells you that it is time. When it does, trust your feeling, and obey without hesitation. Timing is all important. If you have not learnt to discriminate between your persona misleading you and your Impersonal instincts by now, it would be pointless for you to continue. Take this opportunity – it might never come again!"

February 3rd

The last few days had passed peacefully and I had enjoyed the chance to wind down and be completely alone for a change. I had neither seen nor been seen by anyone. There had not been a single whisper from the Inner voice to reassure me about my fate, but I hadn't really needed it. I could feel the benevolent presence of the Impersonal power with me at all times. There were no surprises, no confrontations and no challenges. I was being allowed this period of total relaxation because today was "the" day. I don't know how I knew it, I just did. I knew that my time would be sometime during the next twenty-four hours, so I started to make preparations for later on that evening. I was a little worried about where to locate a second mirror. There was already one at hand, inside the door to the large fitted wardrobe in the bedroom. I had reached the conclusion that I would have to go along to another cabin, as they were of a standard design, and "borrow" a corresponding mirror. I ruled out talking to the park management. My request would sound so peculiar that I cringed with embarrassment at the thought of making my requirement public. I began to think about the task ahead of me. What would come from sitting down in between two mirrors? My comfortable little view of the universe, with its neat little restrictions on reality, had well and truly been shattered. Now reality had become something which was constantly challenging my ideas and beating down the barriers I had set up to govern my way of behaving.

I turned my thoughts to the practical problem of obtaining the second mirror. A rather simple but cunning idea sprang to mind. I would take a walk down to the lodge where I would claim that I had lost my key. Then I'd get the cabin numbers deliberately mixed up and hopefully be handed the one I required. (I did not relish the idea of breaking into an empty cabin and would not have felt comfortable doing so.) The first problem would be identifying a cabin that nobody was renting, or at least one where the occupants were out for the day. I put on my hiking boots and went for a walk. Once again it was fair weather. The clear skies and clean mountain air had been a bonus over the last few days. I had not felt as fit and well for a long time.

I came across the nearest cabin over to the south. It was number 19 and it looked quiet, but whether it was occupied or not it was difficult to tell. I approached cautiously at first, thinking of excuses should I be observed and challenged about my sneaking around. I pictured myself attempting to explain myself away, "Oh, sorry. I thought that it was mine – they all look the same from the outside don't they?" I imagined the nervous laugh that would follow – I was a bad liar. I knocked at the door with no idea of what I might say should someone come to open it. Thankfully, there was no reply, so I crept furtively around the side of the building and peered in through the window. It appeared to be unoccupied. I could not help but feel a little like a criminal as I carried on down the path. When I eventually reached the lodge, I came across an extraordinary stroke of luck. There was no-one in attendance. The board with the large numbered keys hanging from it was just behind the counter. I glanced around me and reached out. I had made a mistake. The key to the chosen cabin wasn't there. I had a split second in which to think. I had no alternative but to chance it, take any key, and just hope that it would belong to an unoccupied cabin. I had a strong intuitive feeling to grab the key numbered 21. Without looking around, I took the key from its hook and quickly left the lodge before anyone had time to return to take up their place behind the counter. Outside I took out my map, located Cabin 21 and started on my way up there. Imagine my relief when I read the large sign which was nailed to the door. It read:

"TEMPORARILY CLOSED FOR REPAIRS"

"Another lucky break," I thought, as once inside, I began unscrewing the full length mirror which hung heavily from the wardrobe door. Of course, I still had the possible problem of being spotted as I walked back to my own cabin, but the chances were against it. Firstly, I didn't have that far to go and secondly, it was mostly under the cover of the sequoia forest where I hadn't encountered a soul ever since I had arrived. I left the key to the cabin in the door, and tucking the mirror under my arm, the reflective side turned in towards me, I made off in the direction of my cabin.

I closed the door behind me with a great feeling of relief. There were few terrors which upset me more than social embarrassment. The thought of all my recent encounters and the fear that I had experienced seemed infinitely preferable than being stopped in the woods by a curious forest ranger!

I took the mirror into the bedroom and leant it against the wall. Before setting up the mirrors, I decided to cook myself a light supper. As I sat to eat my meal, I imagined that I was a condemned man in prison. I knew that death was considered a way out by many people and I also had the recent memory of my friend who had decided to put a gun to his head one day, as a constant reminder that there were people who were actually prepared to go that far. I recognised my situation as an opportunity to find freedom in the heart of life and that that was the way things were meant to be. I had changed a great deal over the past few weeks and could hardly recognise my old self. I was far removed from the self-indulgent man I had become over the years.

I have always been afraid to give myself the chance to be victorious, or to describe myself as a winner. For as long as I can remember, I have suffered from chronic guilt which was utterly baseless as far as I knew. Now I recognised this trait as yet another power play between the "me" I was learning was my true identity and the "mask" or so called "persona" which I was in the process of discarding. I remembered the original definition which the Impersonal friend had given me in one of our early encounters: "persona – mask or that which covers the real". I suspected that now was my chance to remove that mask through my own efforts no matter how painful the process might be. It was too late for alternatives. I had already sentenced myself to succeed. From this moment on, I was determined to accept nothing but the best. Until the arrival of the Impersonal friend in my life, I was always willing to accept mediocrity, I suppose because I had been taught that it was almost impolite to wish for ultimate success. (Perhaps it was a result of spending too many years living in England!) Now, out of habit I had always seemed to aim for a merely adequate experience of life. I thought for a moment about something I had read which summed up my mood. It went:

"You get from life what you give."

With a great sense of purpose, I strode into the bedroom and spent the next half hour setting up the mirrors. When they were eventually in the correct position, exactly six feet apart and directly facing each other, I stepped in between them and began to study my reflection. To my surprise, I immediately began to feel ill. My head started aching and I felt nauseous. I looked up at the pale, bewildered expression staring back at me. Something was drastically wrong. I quickly stepped out from between the mirrors and sat down on the bed, rubbing my eyes and thinking hard. "My god," I thought, when I realised that the mirrors were not in the right position. I estimated them to be approximately facing north-east to south-west. I hurriedly pulled one of them well away from the other and rested it against the bed. I ran into the living room and grabbed my car keys from my coat pocket. Tucked in between the windscreen and the top of the dashboard in my car, was a small compass. I took it and rushed back inside the cabin. I had been a complete fool to forget my instructions. No excuse. No time for fruitless recriminations. I just had to go on. Ten minutes later and the two mirrors were standing in position. The moment I sat down cross-legged on the floor facing West, I held the impression that I was inside a corridor which stretched out into infinity. These two ordinary mirrors that, by their very nature could only represent illusion and *reflect* reality had turned the rules around completely. What was now presented to me was an endless world full of infinite possibilities. From here on in, I was in unchartered territory. Things began to happen rapidly. My reflection was starting to separate itself from the glass – it was already standing. I watched, as it turned and began a slow, bobbing trot. The mirror seemed to be distorted in such a way, that I could now see an infinite number of tiny "sitting Buddha" images of myself stretching out in front of me. It was strange that, confronted as I was by so many visible reflections of myself, it was only the first one, directly in front of me that was imbued with a life of its own. The rest were like drifting shadows: unchosen, unregarded, unimportant.

As the "runner" carried on forwards and inwards, it "pushed" all of the other images out to the far edges of the corridor, carving a path for itself straight ahead. I held the opinion that each mirror image had the same potential and as many as I could see, were the possible paths I could take. I allowed myself to go with the "runner" and to embrace its view as it carried me deeper into its world with each step. On and on I strode with a graceful even pace, running through a dark corridor just as I had done in my dream. In fact, everything had taken on a dreamlike quality. Every time I tried focusing on anything in particular, my sight would blur over and I soon discovered that the best way of looking at things was not to try. I would just relax my eyes and allow myself to be shown this new world.

The tunnel came to an abrupt end. I was out in the open air now surrounded by the most glorious park land. I quickly became overcome by a magnificent display of colour which was so extraordinarily vivid that it made me feel as though I had been seeing the world in black and white up until now. All around me were bright borders planted with every possible colour and variety of flower. Great patches of short-stemmed, crimson rosettes ringed by tall-stemmed, deep ultramarine blue star-shaped flowers appeared in angular borders all around me. Further ahead was a profusion of long, wide arrangements of many variations of colour and shape of plant. Bell-shaped purple blooms contrasted with deep golden pansies, which appeared to be like perfect circles from a distance although they actually possessed five petals which were quite irregular. Large, fat, round heads of orange chrysanthemums grew impossibly close together, giving the impression of a solid unbroken block of colour. Intense scarlet tulip heads danced against the lush cropped green. An unusual short-stemmed alpine ringed all the groups of flowers forming a thin white line drawn quite expertly, creating a rather complicated pattern of repeated interlocking motifs, giving the impression that the whole park had been landscaped by Escher and coloured with the palette of Matisse. It stretched out before me as far as I could see. I had a strange sensation that the earth was falling away beneath my feet, as if, had I ceased to keep moving, then I would have sunk through the soft ground in a gradual downward motion. I was aware of a very slight temptation to allow this to happen but I ignored the feeling, running in a curious zig-zag movement in order to remain on the smooth, green path. By now, I had complete control over my body, which had previously been restricted to simple movements such as turning my head and moving my fingers.

Abruptly the scenery around me changed and I was now a solitary individual running beside an ocean along a beach covered in pale yellow sand. Behind me and to my left there were high sweeping sand dunes backed by a powder blue sky and dotted with spiky grasses. I noticed that the sand was unmarked by the footprints of either people or animals. I felt as though I had wandered into a living painting. On my right waves of blue-green water splashed solidly around my ankles never leaving them wet. I could not tell whether the tide was coming in or out. The air was completely soundless. Even the soft pad, pad of my feet was felt rather than heard. About twenty yards away, standing alone and unsupported, was what seemed to be a doorway in the middle of this surreal landscape. However, on closer inspection, it revealed itself to be a tall, narrow mirror tilted slightly to reflect only sky. I went over and stood directly before it. From where I now stood, it reflected the top half of me, the cloudless blue sky behind my head and the thinnest sliver of light, which was a morning sun – just touching the bottom rim of the mirror's edge. My first impression, that of it being a doorway was correct. As I stood staring into it, it began to mist over. All the reflected shapes were running into each other until it showed nothing except a thin, colourless light. I reached out my hand. It met with no resistance, just simply disappeared up to my elbow. I withdrew my arm sharply wondering if I might still be intact. I remembered reading "Alice Through the Looking Glass". What would I find inside the mirror? Tweedledum and Tweedledee! I suppressed a nervous giggle. "Humpty Dumpty sat on a wall, Humpty Dumpty had a great fall" – I kept repeating this ridiculous nursery rhyme over and over, faster and faster like a merry-go-round that had gone out of control – "All the king's horses and all the king's men, couldn't put Humpty together …."

I thought that I was going insane as yet another voice started to laugh hysterically. Pretty soon there was a chorus of different voices all shouting out equally loudly and persistently. I wasn't going insane. Instead, I was being allowed a glimpse at just how many coats the persona could wear. Some of those outfits were familiar to me. For instance, I could distinguish my mother's voice, and my wife's, amongst all the calling, singing and whispering that was going on. Several of the voices were my own, but they were all making contradictory statements and all seemed to be representative of different moods. Suddenly, the reason for this bizarre identity parade became quite apparent. Not one "character" stood out from the other. You see, none of them were the real me. By this time my nose was just a centimetre away from the "mirror", which had taken the form of a fluctuating silver mist; I had unknowingly moved closer to what lay on the other side. My right arm, belly and feet felt warm while I was standing on a beach where a cold but static wind was "blowing" around me. Without turning round I took one step and found myself back in my cabin standing just outside the bedroom door. I looked around me, then turned and peered into the bedroom through the gap in the half open door. The two mirrors stood face to face just as I had left them. I had a sense that things were not quite right. When I went to open this door I realised what it was. The doorknob was on the right hand side of the door instead of the left as it had been before. Correspondingly, the hinges too were over to the left. Evidence that everything in the cabin had been reversed was everywhere. The figures on the clock were back to front, like the joke ones that you can buy. The long, spidery second hand ticked loudly in an anti-clockwise direction. I opened the window in the living room, only this time it swung outwards from the right hand side, whereas previously its hinges were on the left next to the curtains which had changed colour, pattern and cloth. Incidentally, they were as equally hideous as the ones they had replaced. I looked out at the orange-red remains of a sunset slashing the eastern sky where the sun had risen every day since I had been here.

I set about investigating the many anomalies in and around the cabin. For instance, hot water ran from the cold tap and vice-versa. The higher the number on the electric cooker the less heat was produced. I boiled a kettle on the zero mark. The TV would change to any channel except the one on the dial working backwards. For instance, I could view Channel 1 if I pressed 10 on the remote control. Correspondingly 9 meant 2, 8 meant 3 etc. I soon gave up with the TV set and all the other electrical appliances. These things were bad enough back in the real world after all and were merely irritating rather than frightening. I sat watching the clock moving backwards whilst simultaneously glancing out of the window to see the sun sinking heavily over the eastern side of the mountains, and grew uneasy. I had an idea. I rushed into the bedroom and picked up the compass I had used to position the mirrors. I held it up to the open window where I could feel the hot, still air as the temperature outside was slowly rising and the night grew closer. It did nothing more than spin haphazardly around failing to stop at any particular point long enough for me to take an accurate reading. I tapped it repeatedly, waggled it around uselessly in the air and finally gave it a fairly hefty bang on the window ledge before I gave up and flung it half way across the room. It hit the sofa and fell down between the cushions. It was then that I thought of my car. If I drove far enough away would things decide to set themselves to rights? What if I drove out of the gates of the resort altogether?

Where did this world begin and end?

It was a pleasant surprise to find that my Cherokee was working and in the normal way. Forward meant forward and reverse meant reverse. Fast was fast, and slow was slow. Without bothering to pack anything I began to drive carefully down the wide mountain path.

Have you ever had the feeling when you've been staring at something for a long time, it suddenly changes? A good example is the famous optical illusion of a picture that can either be a vase or the profiles of two people looking at each other. You might start off looking at the faces when your perspective suddenly and imperceptibly shifts, and you find that the only shape that you can now determine is that of the vase. I've had similar experiences when I've been travelling by rail for a long time and for a moment it seems as though the train is travelling backwards. I would usually blink at that point and my vision would return to normal. So far as I knew, something similar was happening to me now as my view of a downward hill would shift to that of a rough mountain track climbing upwards, ending up at my cabin every time. This went on for some time before I finally got out of the car five hundred yards or so away from the park gates and decided to walk the rest of the way. "Good," I said out loud to myself, "still going down." After walking for about ten minutes I found myself approaching the cabin from the north-east path (at least I had come to recognise it as north-east up until now).

I was back in the cabin. I had given up all thoughts of escaping back to the "real" world in an orthodox fashion when I had what I thought was a brainwave. I ran back into the bedroom. The mirrors stood upright like two sentinels. I tapped them both, but they were solid. I sat down between them as I had done before and met with a single reflection only. This was impossible! I bowed my head and rubbed my neck, hard.

"This is what I meant when I said that there was no way to go back, only forward. You must face whatever situation now arises. I cannot help you anymore. You have the strength to utilize the Impersonal power, I can guarantee that. So befriend yourself in this crucial time. Here you will meet with your enemy. I can say nothing more than that, when you have come here to do what you have to do, your world will be put to rights. Do not be alarmed. It is time for you to become the Impersonal being."

I still felt I needed some reassurance that I would know what to do.

"I am unable to give you any clues. This is your affair entirely and it is your responsibility to be decisive about how you will deal with events to come. I myself do not know what form your confrontation will take, but I do believe that you are ready to face that which has been the source of all your pain throughout your life and destroy it. If you should choose to avoid the inevitable you will only make matters worse, but if you draw the personal powers out into the open, you have a chance. That is the secret. To be responsible for what you have created and bring it under control."

There followed an unbearable silence when I knew that I might never hear the Impersonal voice again. In that moment I knew what complete isolation meant.

CHAPTER EIGHT

Dusk to Dust

In my own way, I was declaring myself ready and prepared for the "showdown" when I stood up and decided to take a walk outside. I was impatient in wanting whoever or whatever was after me to make itself known. Yet to my great frustration, I was allowed to take my walk unmolested. My foe was choosing its moment carefully. The time came after I had returned to my cabin and had taken a nap. I was awoken abruptly by a thunderous crashing on the cabin door. It was dark outside and a fierce wind was howling around the front of the building. The wooden doorframe was rattling, giving the impression that it was made from matchsticks and that it would collapse around me at any moment. I knew that my growing fears would inevitably accelerate into an uncontrollable panic, should it continue for much longer. There was an inhuman howling outside as the door was hammered at repeatedly. Knowing instinctively that I was under siege, I thought that the best thing to do was to get out and into the woods. So, very slowly, I inched my way over to the kitchen where I planned to crawl out of the window above the sink. I had to pass the door which was arching out from its hinges and shaking as if possessed. Everything looked and moved something like a Disney cartoon, and everything was twisting and jerking in a variety of impossible movements. I shook my head and blinked. Things would return to normal for a fleeting moment before all the rules were thrown aside once more and the whole place would rapidly return to chaos. Furniture would appear and disappear at will, manifesting in bizarre places. Sometimes one piece of furniture could be seen balancing precariously on top of another. Once I looked and saw a chair and desk occupying the same place at the same time, as if I were looking at a picture covered by a film of tracing paper with objects drawn over it, being flipped back and forth. I found it all strangely hypnotic, so after a while, I decided not to look at, or take seriously anything I was seeing. All that was being done to distract me was done for a purpose. Feeling a little like the sorcerer's apprentice in the midst of all this havoc, I quietly unbolted the kitchen window and scrambled out, falling clumsily to the floor. It was unnerving to notice that this side of the building lay calm and undisturbed while the rest of it groaned and strained in response to the fierce and unremitting assault upon it. I could never in my life have conceived of such a subtle and disorientating form of threat.

Was I mistaken or did the raging wind seem to own a personality? That would explain why it was concentrating on the cabin door. It wanted *me*! As ridiculous as this might sound I knew that it was true when I looked around the side of the building. As I did so, the whole place became absolutely still. I had been "seen". I stared and could almost make out the vague twisted, yet strangely characterless form which inhabited the winds. It was tall – about twelve to fourteen feet or so – and stood up uncomfortably on two satyr-like hind legs. I took all things in, in a split second. I did not wait to study its face as I turned and sped into the woods. I knew it was following me as I ran through the trees. A vicious, searing wind tore past my face at lightning speed. I whimpered each time it caught me, as it felt as though I were being slashed to shreds by giant razorblades. Again and again it attacked, while I ran helter-skelter, until I finally burst out from the trees to find myself standing by the edge of the ravine which overlooked the lake. It was the identical spot where I had undergone my trial the other evening, except that the moon was now on my right. I was not followed, but in a local area amongst the sequoias just in front of me, a tiny storm raged with soundless fury. It was no mistake that I had emerged in this particular spot and immediately recognised that it was to my advantage. I viewed my last few moments of terror with relative calm as I stood catching my breath. Whatever it was that I *almost* saw, now well hidden within the tree trunks, was partly due to my own fear, because the more I fought to bring my panic under control, the less the wind blew. After a while the surrounding woods became still. A man stood in front of me in between two of the tallest trees.

I hadn't noticed his arrival and had not reacted in the slightest at his sudden appearance. It was as though we had been standing there for the whole of eternity. I felt neither frightened nor courageous. There was nothing to be felt, experienced or interpreted. I had let go and the game began to play itself.

I moved slightly and was about to wave and call out to him, but I corrected myself mid-cry. "Oh no," I thought, "this is it." The man was looking directly at me, that much I could tell, although his "face" was absolutely smooth and featureless like a man wearing a stocking mask. He moved closer to me without actually taking steps. I found I could make him keep his distance by refusing to blink.

But inevitably, my eyes watered over and he was right in front of me about five feet away. “What do you want?” I asked. “Why do you pursue me?” He did not answer. I took my chance to study him more closely. He was the same height as me and wore the same clothes, although they possessed a shabby dun colour. The skies were almost completely clear and the bright moon lit up the whole area, myself included, but the creature (for I could no longer consider “it” to be a man in front of me) did not reflect the light. It stood there like a solid shadow, with flesh that looked like it was made from putty. Its face split into a bizarre form of grin, revealing a black, toothless mouth. “You are weak!” it said. “I will defeat you!” The voice was completely devoid of all human emotions and was as nondescript as it could possibly be. Yet it filled me with loathing. I replied with a nervous laugh. My body tensed up waiting for it to physically attack me. However, its approach was far more subtle.

“Why don’t you jump?” it said, glancing over toward the ravine’s edge. “If you’re so powerful, you should come to no harm. Go on – show me. SHOW ME.”

It became encouraged as I followed its stare.

“Prove to me that you are fit to take over. Prove that you are fit to be my master.”

Anger welled up inside me and tears sprang from my eyes. An inward prayer flew upwards from deep within me.

“Help me. Save me from myself.”

I felt frightened and alone and longed to feel the presence of my friend, but I knew that I was on my own. I began to cry, quietly at first because I felt ashamed, but there was no way I could prevent myself from sobbing out loud. I didn’t mind abandoning my ridiculous social considerations, I was on my own anyway, and I let out a long, loud wail.

After a while the tears subsided and I closed my eyes. From where my anger sprang I had no idea, but I turned and glared at the loathsome thing which stood there so calmly, watching me with disdain. How dare it consider itself anything to do with me? How dare it judge me? How dare it even look at me? It had no right to even exist. I surprised myself as, with a sudden cry of rage, I lunged at the creature. My hands gripped the thin, smooth throat and, screaming at the top of my voice, I repeatedly smashed the head against the hard earth. I squealed with delight as the hairless skull made a cracking sound as it hit a jagged rock. I thrashed around on the ground, crazed with glee as bones broke and sinews snapped. I failed to notice that, in my frenzy, I was moving dangerously close to the ravine's edge. It didn't take me long to realise that firstly the creature had slipped quite effortlessly from my grasp and regained its form (it showed no sign of injury whatsoever) and secondly, half of me was hanging over the edge of the cliff. I looked up, my legs dangling helplessly, with nothing in front of me to grasp. I saw that the creature was standing over me and that it was likely to push me back if I attempted to pull myself up. Alternatively, I was unsuccessful in finding a foothold, in order to climb down. Below, I could hear the heavy slopping sound of the water – there was no way out.

It was a strange sensation – as if part of me had just fallen away or decided to give in. Never letting my eyes leave the dark figure before me, I lifted up my hands and allowed myself to fall backwards, whilst simultaneously (and impossibly) lunging forward. Using the muscles of my stomach and my elbows as a lever, I shot up into standing position, landing about four feet away from the edge. The creature had since made a silent and rapid retreat, and now stood close to the forest edge. Continuing the momentum, I lowered my head, charged and slammed it full force in the guts. With a startled shriek, it flew backwards for several yards, smashed into a tree and slumped to the ground. It was dead – I was sure. I raced over to find nothing there, save a pile of dead leaves and branches which I kicked around violently in my frustration at finding no body. My head jerked around to the left and right, but there was no sign of my foe. So far it had not managed to destroy me, but I knew that it had only retreated in order to resume its attack when it was ready. I waited for a while before heading off back to my cabin. As I alternated between walking and running, I gradually became aware that I was charged with the most incredible energy. It was shooting up from out of the ground, travelling up through my ankles, rippling along my calf muscles and thighs, up through my spine until it eventually reached my shoulders, where it rested like a back-pack, releasing power to every other part of my body. The back of my neck was pulsating with it. My chest moved in and out like a machine of war. My body was on fire, burning like my own raging anger. I listened carefully to detect whether or not I was alone. My senses had been "gathered up" and were now concentrated around the area of my solar plexus. I had access to a power which was not allowing itself to be limited by the feebleness of my own body.

I imagined myself moving through the forest like a cougar, stalking its prey. Several times I felt like calling out to my enemy and issuing a challenge, but there was no need – it knew where I was, just outside my cabin in fact. I was reluctant to go inside. Outside in the dark, among the sequoias I felt no fear. From now on, I would be the hunter and I would seek out and destroy any part of me which

I considered to be useless or a menace to my wellbeing. Out here in the night, I would really see what I was made of. I turned my back on Cabin 12A and made off down the mountain track.

Initially, I viewed the lake with some suspicion. Water was not an element that I could well deal with, yet at the same time I knew the deep harboured no personal threats. The water plants (I didn't know their names) twisted about on the surface, forming fantastic almost hypnotic shapes before my eyes. They resembled insidious writhing serpents and my mind was full of vivid images of them rising up out of the water, wrapping themselves around me and pulling me down beneath the surface of the lake. Down, down into the deep dark water. I shuddered. I had let my imagination run wild, which was the worst thing that I could have allowed myself to do at that point.

I had presumed that my enemy lay elsewhere. I was wrong. I heard a yell and a splash close by. I looked up, as whatever it was could have only fallen from the top of a tree – an animal perhaps? Still suspecting a trick and with great caution, I went to investigate. I peered, straining my eyes in the moonlight (it was cloud free at that particular moment and very bright) to see if there might be anything struggling in the water. It was then that I remembered the mist and the voice calling out for help, and how it had been an attempt by the persona to convince me that I was in some way responsible for its survival. A sudden feeling of vulnerability swept over me – perhaps I had been tempting providence in visiting the lakeside? I turned just in time to see something smash into me, causing me to lose my balance and fall into the slime at the water's edge, hitting the side of my head on a branch in the process. I had fallen into deep black mud and rapidly began to sink. I struggled to find a grip on the roots that were growing out from the bank, but they were covered in foul-smelling algae that felt like mucous and were totally impossible to grasp. The slime seemed intent on pulling me under. I looked around for help. There was a good chance that I might be heard by a forest ranger on night patrol. I was terrified and attempted to struggle free. Between my yelling and floundering around, I had managed to sink deeper quickly. Not all the forces of nature were on my side.

I recalled the words I had once heard at a lecture. The speaker had used the example of a drowning man, pointing out that a fellow in such a predicament would usually make matters worse for himself by panicking. Consequently, his struggling and splashing around would only succeed in drawing him deeper into the water. Therefore, I ceased my efforts to scramble to safety, although it was difficult for me to accept that to do nothing was the only option open to me – It felt like jumping out of a plane without a parachute!

There was a ghastly sucking noise, as I was being dragged even deeper. I was forced to lay my head back in order to continue breathing. If I were to sink just a few inches further, my mouth and lungs would start to fill up with stinking mud. I remained, it seemed, between the two states of being and not being, of life and death. Never before had I been faced with the fact of my own insignificance and that there were forces which possessed such a malevolent design upon me. My body had become petrified. It was shocked into such a dramatic paralysis at the realisation that it might no longer hold life. I understood vividly what I had caught a glimpse of in my practise of the mirror technique. That is, that my body was merely a vehicle for the indefinable essence of existence I would refer to as "me". My body truly would have no purpose should "I" be unlucky enough to have to depart from it there and then, leaving it to float uselessly on the waters of the lake.

Meanwhile, I was being bombarded with pellets of rolled mud and stones by a scrawny looking creature which had climbed high into the trees above me. It looked similar to the "animal" that I had seen in the wind that had been tearing around my house earlier. It seemed uninterested in taking more violent action toward me. It had probably arrived at the conclusion that I was destined to die in a matter of minutes and simply wished to enjoy the spectacle. It was also fairly obvious that it was deriving tremendous pleasure from the nature of my final defeat. I inclined my head a little so that I could watch the creature that was watching me. It was frighteningly large, perhaps fifteen to twenty feet, skeletal and inhuman in every aspect. It loosely resembled a type of deformed man, possessing a long, flat, bony "head" which was set awkwardly on the shoulders. The two ends were flattened and stretched out lengthways, with highly specialised mouth parts, like those of a manta ray.

"You are right out of the twilight zone, my gross little friend!"

I was neither frightened nor afraid by its appearance or its lack of manners. As if it were aware of just how unimpressed I was, it turned its back to me, moved out to the end of a branch and began to defecate into the water close to my face. While I, unable to move, watched solemnly, wondering how far away I was from my last breath as the water slopped all around me. The creature's vile behaviour merited nothing more than slight interest and did not seem in the least surprising.

I very slowly turned my head to the left to look up at the moon. The move, which I judged to be quite unconscious, was a precaution. Should I die, I did not want such an obscene process to be the last thing that I would witness.

My body had begun to have strange periodic convulsions, which were rapidly increasing both in intensity and frequency, unfortunately disturbing the filth that had begun to accumulate all around me. A loud splash sounded close to my head emitting a particularly foul stench. Still I stared up at the moon. A leaf fell from high above me and fluttered across its implacable face. I wondered if that might be the last thing that my eyes would ever see, but by now it didn't seem to matter. I cared for nothing. I was waiting for some great hand to reach out and turn off the light and in that moment nothing mattered. It didn't matter how I had lived my life; whether or not I had been a success or a failure in any aspect of my life, whether I had been loved or hated or even liked. I had no concern except that for the immediate moment and hoping that the light would keep shining. I had never been ill enough in my life to experience the possibility of dying. I believed that I was too young to worry about such a possibility: how sacred each breath felt, as I lay beneath the skies, remaining as still as I could. One thing I still possessed was hope, even now, even when it seemed as though there was no way to save myself, I still had hope.

So softly was its approach, and so gentle, that at first I mistakenly defined it as my death. As it grew stronger within me, I began to identify its true nature. It was trust!

With an overpowering sense of relief, I surrendered myself to the Impersonal power, as I had done in my dream and made my escape in the most remarkable fashion.

I focused my attention on a tree a few yards in front of me, concentrated hard. Then, in a violent spinning motion, I literally drilled myself out from the mud bank and shot forward onto the shore, arriving at the feet of my aggressor. I had landed in a crouching position adopting an ape-like stance. My arms hung loosely swinging by my side, dripping with water and slime. I slowly raised my head and stared hard into the creature's face, which became revoltingly distorted as it attempted to register the surprise and shock which it must have felt. It had obviously been alarmed by my rapid recovery. After a brief moment's hesitation it began to back off very cautiously, walking in a strange crab-like manner, never taking its "eyes" off me for an instant. In a moment it had broken free from my gaze, scuttled sideways into the safety of the woods and was gone. Thrilled by the shock of the cold water and my seeming invincibility, I gave chase only to find myself pursuing shadows. The creature could obviously appear and disappear at will.

As I wandered aimlessly around among the great trees for a while, I began to see the disadvantage of pursuing an enemy that was bound to pursue me. I would merely end up wasting time and energy. I began to think tactically. It would come after me wherever I was, so I quickly made my way up to the ridge to make my stand in the place where I knew I would have the greatest advantage over my opponent.

Moments later and I found myself sitting, cross-legged, in the exact same spot that I had done five nights ago when I had nothing more alarming to contend with than a frightened animal. My back was to the ravine's edge, so as to allow me a one hundred and eighty degree view of the forest edge in front of me. In such a position, nothing could make its approach without being seen, unless it had the ability to climb up the sheer wet stone behind me – a possibility I did not discount. I had a commanding view from where I sat. The rock jutted out from the fairly straight line on my right in an odd angular shape, before returning to the same level. The forest gradually curved away to my left, where visibility was clear. Once again, nothing could get close to me if it came from that direction, without being seen from a long way off. I allowed my mind to sink into my breath where it rested, cloaked in power.

The importance of this manoeuvre had not escaped me. I knew that my creature (for it was obvious that it belonged to me and was therefore my responsibility) would have to make its approach soon.

When the final confrontation came it was at 3.30 am. In that hour my foe came to me. It began by taunting me with threats and abuse. Having complete knowledge of my weaknesses it tried one gambit after another in its attempt to undermine my confidence. The realisation it was a "personal" attack that referred to many aspects of my life, helped at the most difficult times. It made repeated references to the innumerable mistakes I had made throughout my life. This succeeded in causing me to feel a great deal of guilt which was the most painful part of the assault I had to endure. My persona taunted me with its whole repertoire of tricks and illusions. It possessed a comprehensive knowledge of all my weaknesses, as my Impersonal friend had once said, "it was the root cause of them."

I could see nothing, but could hear, coming from the direction of the trees, a series of voices, each one belonging to the many different people I had known in my life – some of whom I had loved and some I had hated. Either way, they were intensely distracting. At times, due to an excess of emotion, I was tempted to respond. But I was determined to hold fast even when I heard the voice of my own son calling out to me in a most pitiful and yet accusative manner, claiming that I had deserted him. Again and again, he begged me for an explanation, which of course, “him” not really being “him”, I could not give. The pressure upon me increased as my ex-wife, her family and all my friends joined in. They all managed to sound so hurt and aggrieved by my actions, and I longed to stand up and tell them just how wrong they were. I especially needed to go out and find my son, however illogical it seemed, and tell him for the first time in his adult life, my side of the story. It was something I had dreamed of doing for years, but “he” was beginning to express “his” hatred for me by now. He was neither crying nor pleading with me, but screaming and shouting, declaring that he never wanted to see me again.

From out of the trees flew a Miami Dolphins football jacket, which was instantly recognisable because of its vivid orange and green colours, tailored to fit a four-year-old. I had given my son an identical jacket on the last birthday he spent with me. I reached over to pick it up. I wondered at it. It looked like new. Just as I had it in my grasp, there was a great crashing sound of branches being broken, as something like a wild animal moved through the tallest of the trees above me. I knew then that my adversary had gained some kind of advantage over me through my mistake. From looking up, my gaze travelled down the tree trunks, but I saw nothing. I looked again at the ground in front of me where the jacket had been thrown. It had vanished. The clouds covered the moon’s face again, turning off the lights, leaving me in an unholy blackness. My recent encounter down upon the shores of that great lake with all those evil plants, which seemed as if they were living ropes intent on dragging their victims down into hell itself and which had almost succeeded in ending my life, had unnerved me more than I realised. I had suddenly become afraid of the dark.

I knew that I had brought it upon myself by reaching for that damned jacket. There was a sudden rustle of leaves directly in front of me, which was probably the same grotesque manifestation that had sat to watch me drown only a short while ago, but I couldn't count on it. One thing I was quite sure about, in the same way I had to remain still until the right moment when I had lain gasping for air in that ghastly mud, so I had to remain on the exact spot where I was now sitting, even if an entire army came rushing towards me.

The voices, the child's jacket, all were tricks played on me in order to lure me from my place of power.

The voice echoed throughout the darkness.

"You did well down at the lake. You learnt that you possessed limited powers only – and it was death that showed this to you." It went on. "You've learnt to trust in the Impersonal power and so escaped death itself. Have you not realised the power you have managed to harness? Just imagine yourself – separated from the rest of humanity – a superman, a leader of men. No longer a timid, frightened individual whose life is dictated to by others!"

It was unmistakably the sound of my friend which was booming out across the lake. I could not accurately determine from which direction it was coming. The rhetoric continued and I listened, but only with my ears … it was failing to reach the inner me which I refer to as Impersonal. There was only one answer as to why not. The sound I was hearing was not my "inner" friend and I became terrified. The moment I was touched by fear I was on a helter-skelter, hurtling downwards at increasing speed with no way to stop the gathering momentum. I began to lose consciousness – was I dying? Was I descending into the domain of Lucifer? Eventually I passed out.

I was still sitting in my special place, but I was confused. How long had I blacked out? It had seemed like hours, but my watch confirmed that it had only been a matter of a few minutes.

A series of doubts entered my mind.

Was I sitting in the right place? Perhaps it was time to move? Was I doing the right thing? By declaring war on a part of myself that had just as much claim on me as my so-called Impersonal friend and had accompanied me throughout my entire life? After all, the "inner" friend had only made itself known a short time ago. And as for the Impersonal powers! Why did I not possess complete comprehension of them and their importance from the very moment I was born? I had been told that they were my birth-right. If that had been the case, so much of my pain and suffering would have been avoided. My friend had tricked me as to its intentions. It had lured me into an unfamiliar world from which there was no escape and it would probably go back on all its promises, revealing itself to be the real enemy. I recalled the first words it ever spoke to me … "I am neither alien nor mysterious." It was quite likely to be both.

I saw the chaos in which I had made a home for myself. I saw how chaos had become something which I could both accept and believe in. I saw the pendulum swing from one extreme to the other, from euphoria to despair, from enthusiasm to bitterness, from order to disorder, from forward motion to retrograde motion. Chaos was the biblical Hell.

Had I been deceived by Satan? Had I myself become satanic?

"Hell is in man," I shouted out loud.

I knew that the abyss was directly behind me. Should I turn and face it? Were the things I feared, my salvation and those I loved, the veiled face of evil? Should I reverse everything I believed in to become Impersonal? Church bells were ringing in my ears, the bells I used to hear as a child.

"The Father, the Son and the Holy Ghost, Amen."

"Hey! What's the difference between a good nun and a bad nun?"

"I dunno, what is the difference between a good nun and a bad nun?"

"A good nun says Amen, and a bad nun says ah, men!"

I had completely cracked up and laughed so loudly and so long that I had ached all over. As my boyish laughter echoed around my head, I began remembering the sound of the church bells again, when my mum first took me to St. Mary's, much against my will. Church going was considered sissy amongst my peers – and I wasn't so keen on it myself! Much to my surprise and embarrassment, I started to cry, as the bells clashed and thundered above, despite my best friend's attempt to cheer me up with his manic and hilarious impersonation of Quasimodo, as he ran totally unrestrained around the pews, leaping onto them and shouting at the top of his voice, "The bells, the bells!" It might have worked, but his "unforgivable" activities were eventually put a stop to by the combined efforts of his flamboyantly-attired mother and the poor Parish Priest, who looked as if he were tackling Count Dracula himself.

Still those bells clashed and thundered above my head. Great metal giants smashing into each other – there were no nice tunes, no nice words. I was hurt and frightened. I turned to my mother. "If the Baby Jesus keeps hearing the bells all the time, how will he sleep?"

My mother hit me, hard on the back of the head, and I began to cry and struggle until I finally broke free from her grasp. I ran away, barely seeing where I was going through my tears. I ran and ran, ran from the noise and the pain. Why had my mum hit me, why?

"Suffer the little children to come unto me."

It wasn't true. God hit you. Jesus hit you. Every time I did something "bad", somebody would hit me, and I couldn't help but do things wrong the whole time.

I ran all the way to my secret camp, where I wouldn't get hurt. It was right in the middle of an old derelict piece of ground that the local gossips and worried parents were always nagging us kids to stay away from, going on about the unexploded bombs left over from the war, but I didn't care. People were afraid to go there. They were all scared – but I wasn't.

"You are not my friend," I called out in the darkness. "You are an imposter. You are not from the Impersonal world and I will no longer listen to you. You have lost."

I hadn't noticed the two long, thin charcoal black hands had a fierce grip on my upper arms. As I spoke they immediately relinquished their hold on me and dropped uselessly beside a tall dark amorphous body, which seemed as though it had suddenly been filleted on the spot as it crumpled into a revolting mass of fleshy sludge before my keenly- staring eyes. It lay draped over a convenient piece of semi-upright timber, like one of Dali's soft watches. I even checked the "legs" for ants! I took up a nearby stick and poked at the body. It felt like a dead jelly fish, and although it was soft, it was resilient and possessed a faint but discernible and regular pulse. Without letting my eyes leave the "body", I looked around. I had been dragged along the ground for almost two feet, back towards the direction of the forest. Remaining on the ground, I managed a quick shuffle on my backside to where I had originally been sitting. It was then that I noticed that my head was clear again. The bells had stopped ringing, the voice had stopped talking and once again the creature had evaded capture as it spread itself out like an oil slick and simply disappeared into the ground before I had time to blink.

There are two points around about the top of my shoulder blades (from where you'd expect cupid's wings to sprout) which felt as though they were on fire. Imagine that those two points were being opened, releasing the energy that was contained within my body so that it might pour out and downwards, coursing down my back in two parallel lines, literally riveting me to the earth. This is the only way I can describe the sensations that I was feeling. Down through the hard rock the two poles bored, as if they were drilling for oil. Most of the time they ran straight down, but sometimes they would swerve to various degrees around the compass, but whichever, they would always remain exactly parallel to each other. I was fascinated by the process, yet completely unafraid. At one point, I saw my enemy moving rapidly along the forest edge, this time cloaked in a strange colourless garment that resembled a monk's robe and cowl. I was forced to sit and watch, bolted to the ground as I was. Its mysterious mockingly "spiritual" covering and its disconcerting gliding motion succeeded once again, in provoking me into attempting to manoeuvre myself into what I considered was an attack position. I left the ground and found myself squatting; I recognised I had made another mistake as I was unable to rise to my feet even when I tried). The "back-pack" of power had been attempting to unite itself with some great reserve of energy, stored deep in the planet about which I knew nothing. The energy of the earth's two poles that had been following instincts, of which I could not conceive, had been weakened the minute I moved and I began to sway precariously from side to side. My adversary responded without hesitation, floating toward me, its height increasing as it approached. It was well over fifteen feet tall and it attempted to make me lose my balance by sweeping its robe over my head.

I had won before using the simple resourcefulness and fearlessness of a child. However, a child needs the protection of a parent. Was I not instinctively searching for the bond that exists with the earth, the parent of all its inhabitants? I felt a strong compulsion to sit back down, although the idea of doing battle from such a position seemed ludicrous and the total opposite of what I should be doing. My body was screaming at me to "let go", to stop "thinking", and to allow myself to fall gently back into my original position. I quickly realised that I couldn't contend with being at war with myself, while there was such a dangerously malevolent force outside of me, and its moves were sudden. It was nearly on top of me – when I folded my legs neatly up under me and sat back, leaving the Impersonal power to continue its search deep beneath me. I very quickly learned how to defend myself. Merely by raising an arm or a hand, I was able to keep the monkish apparition at bay. I learned that by inclining my head slightly to the left and pointing with my three middle fingers, I could stop the creature from advancing, as well as forcing it to move backwards or side to side. After a while it gave up once again and retreated into the safety of the forest, leaving me unmolested for an immeasurable time. I say immeasurable because time ceased to be an absolute or dominating factor, as the two poles of power were travelling along pathways known only to themselves, to an incalculable depth where they eventually struck the mother lode. At this point, any attempt to describe what I experienced would be impossible. But being someone who must analyse everything, I had to try. I was inside. The best metaphor to use would be that of an embryo floating inside the womb of its mother, for that's how I felt. In that immeasurable time, I knew everything; the earth gave up all her secrets to me and I knew then how humanity was underestimating her. She knew how to deal with the creatures who crawled about on her surface should they threaten her existence. She was watching, or more correctly, feeling every thought, vibration, intention and was in control. There was much more. It was indescribable. If I attempted to do so, I would probably sound foolish to the majority of people. I would be accused of hallucinating or imagining what was happening. The understanding I was having went far beyond the realm of the human mind. That is why it was indescribable. I once watched a Donahue TV show, where the subject matter was "Life after death experiences". The panel of guests who claimed that they had had such an experience found great comfort in one another. They all expressed that they no longer feared death after their experience. As for the audience: they were apparently inspired and comforted by what they had heard, but there were voices of dissent, claiming that these people were hallucinating. There was no way their minds were going to be changed on only hearsay evidence. So what I was now privileged to witness and to know would be something that I knew I would be keeping to myself. This is the difference in knowing and believing.

The flow of energy reversed dramatically. When the process had been completed, my parent released me from her hold. The grim figure which was still haunting me, watching me from a relatively safe distance (from its point of view rather than mine) returned from the shelter of the sequoias. Its attempts to shatter my nerves were relentless but futile, as I sat calmly waiting for the right time to deal with it. It did not try to approach me again. At times it appeared almost comic, as it turned to hurl some disgusting form of abuse at me. However, while it still existed it was no laughing matter. After a while it grew weary and was actually stooping as I eventually walked over to it.

"Come with me," I said in a friendly voice.

I think that it believed that I held some compassion for it, which is why it came out from the trees so obediently and walked over to the ravine with me. It appeared a great deal less sinister in the thin yellow light, which had just begun to spread across the horizon. It wore a mournful expression, which utterly failed to deceive me, although it tried to present a more threatening look from time to time. We stopped and stood face to face, the abyss to my right.

"You expect me to pity you, don't you, after all your attempts to kill me, not just tonight but all the pain you have caused me throughout my life?"

It did not reply. I looked into the creature's eyes, for I could see now that it had eyes of a sort. They were grey or dun-coloured like the rest of it, and not moist like a human's, but dry and leathery – and there were no eyelids. "Behind those eyes is a vacuum," I thought. It was then that I knew that it was not alive. You can't kill something that is dead already, so, feeling no emotion whatsoever, I simply grabbed the thing by the neck, lifted it up off its feet (it weighed no more than a paper bag) and threw it over the ravine's edge into the water below.

In an instant, I was back in my cabin. I went behind the mirror that faced westward and stepped through, back into my world. The dawn light showed reassuringly through the east window. I was ready to breathe a sigh of relief when

I was disturbed by a faint scratching sound, like the scrape of a fingernail across a blackboard. I turned around and checked the two mirrors. A tiny pinprick of light showed in the west facing mirror, the one I had just stepped through, like a diamond. I knelt down and, closing one eye, I looked in to see the world between two mirrors and close to, on the other side, a huddled creature was crouching, its head bowed so low that it almost lay in the dirt. A bony claw, shaped like a man's but possessing too many joints on the fingers to be human, was reaching toward the mirror's silver back. With a hefty boot I kicked it to pieces, then turned and violently flung the other mirror into the wall. They exploded into a thousand fragments, which crashed to the floor, leaving a mist of diamond dust floating in the air around me. The gateway to the Impersonal world had been annihilated. Without bothering about the mess, I waded through the shattered glass which covered the floor, flung myself on my bed and crying tears of relief and exhaustion, fell into a deep sleep.

CHAPTER NINE

Down the Mountain Trail

Philosophy – *"use of reason and argument in search for truth and knowledge of reality ..."*
Experience – *"personal observation of or involvement with fact or event ..."*

I awoke around about mid-morning, lying face down on the bed, still dressed in my clothes, my feet hanging over the bed weighted by my hiking boots. I stretched my whole body and turned to face the window, so that I might feel the warmth of the sun. I knew it would be chilly outside, so I lay cuddled up in my blanket, boots and all. It couldn't have felt better had I been sunbathing on a Miami beach. For some time, I remained like this, spread out lazily, like a fat contented cat sitting on a window sill, eyes half closed; safe, pampered and completely protected from any harm.

Half an hour later, I threw off the covers, flung the cabin door open and stood framed in the doorway, my hungry lungs pulling in the clean mountain air. The cold numbed my nasal passage and my temples. My forehead felt as though an ice pack were being pressed against it. My chest moved in and out, a precise and powerful machine which was very effectively controlling the whole process. It felt as though I were actually being breathed into rather than labouring away to catch the air. Inside my head, my brain felt as if it had been adjusted in some way – that it had somehow been manoeuvred into its correct position. It was now quite obvious to me that my perception of affairs to date had been seriously distorted. If I had been out of focus, I had since received some fine tuning; I spent some moments wondering how I had survived for so long, blundering around like Mr. Magoo! I held the definite impression that the doorway to this unassuming cabin marked the threshold to a new life, which rolled out before me like the mountain scenery that levelled before my eyes. Was I now the "Impersonal" man?

I went inside to shower after deciding that I would take a walk down the mountain to the lodge for some hot coffee and a cooked breakfast, before preparing to head for home. (I instinctively knew that it was time to leave.) The line belonging to an old and familiar song kept repeating itself over in my head, "if my friends could see me now," as I shuffled around in the bedroom dressed only in a rather shabby dressing gown and my old hiking boots, unavoidably grinding broken glass into the carpet. I nudged some of the larger pieces out of the way in order to reach the wardrobe, where I began to pick out clothes suitable for my drive home, and remove the rest ready for packing. I paused to survey the devastation I had caused. I planned to have a thorough clean up immediately after breakfast.

I stood beneath the shower, my insides burning like cold fire. I bowed my head under the warm spray and closed my eyes. A picture began to form in my mind's eye of myself as a child, who wore my son's beautiful face when he was just four years old – the last time I had seen him – seated on the forest floor beneath a giant sequoia, which was decked out as if it were a Christmas tree. Plump little fingers were busy unwrapping one brightly decorated package after another.

Inside each one were moments in time, presented to him as a life to be enjoyed. I saw the light of simple appreciation spread across his face. My heart was opening up to the love I held there for my boy, who I had spent such a short time with before he had been snatched from me, so suddenly and so cruelly. My tears mingled with the water. I had not allowed myself to feel that particular grieving for a long time; but they were tears of acceptance.

As I towelled myself dry, I caught a glimpse of my face in the shaving mirror – I was starting to show a beard!

I walked briskly down the mountain trail, and for the first time since I had woken, I remembered my friend. Immediately I became overwhelmed by an elaborate cocktail of emotions, ranging from excitement and pride, to gratitude and intense longing to share my feeling with my teacher and guide. Beyond the exhilaration of the moment I desperately needed the simple feeling of not being alone.

As I walked down the forest trail I gradually became aware of the difference in my physical being, which was a direct result of surrendering myself to the Impersonal powers. The potential inside me was limitless!

A few moments later I became aware that I was not the only one participating in my pleasure. In a similar way in which a particularly grand limousine might silently pull up beside you at a set of lights, and remain almost unnoticed for a while, I gradually became aware that my friend had joined me. He knew and understood and was "pleased" that I was able to be so at home with myself. When my friend spoke his "words" were so close as to almost be indivisible from my own thoughts and sensations. At times, I felt as though I were simply thinking "in-loud", so to speak, rather than being the ardent listener I had been for so many weeks. I also noticed that the sound of my friend's voice was identical to the sound of my own voice, only altered slightly so as to be unrecognisable at first – like something heard through a tape recorder, for instance. It is "you", you can't deny it, yet when you actually listen to it, it sounds totally different from how you hear yourself inside your imagination. It can often be surprising or even a little embarrassing!

Just for the record, I noticed that I had lost a great deal of my original home counties accent to a slightly clipped version of the laid back West coast drawl which had been such a constantly irritating assault upon my ears ever since I had first taken up residence here. Once I realised that the average American storekeeper or bus driver was probably ten times more straightforward and articulate than most English politicians or pundits, I relinquished my criticism of the relative slowness of my neighbours' speech (which I had initially mistaken for lack of intelligence).

I began to wonder if the now familiar sound of my friend's voice was more "me" than me! This shift in perspective of who or what, by strict definition, the "Impersonal" friend was, did not disturb me in the least. In fact it seemed quite logical that if something sprang from some deep part of my being then it would be unsurprising should its surface be marked with my own characteristics. My friend began to speak of the morning and its magic.

"You have faced your hidden fears and have emerged victorious after your confrontation with the persona. You are entitled to feel the way you have been this morning, but do not expect life to continue to be so dramatic and intense. You now have the opportunity to begin to appreciate its simplicity and its unassuming beauty. During your trial, you had to deal with symbols which resulted from the nature of your own personality. The images you saw were neither real nor unreal – those definitions are not relevant when you are describing aspects of the Impersonal world – you were fighting fire with fire, so to speak. What I have done for you is to help free you so that you may carry on with your life without any interference from your persona. You see, firstly I had to identify it, and then, with your co-operation, isolate it. Finally you were required to free yourself from its control alone.

"Now you can see that life is a friend, a guide, and a teacher – even a lover – and that it is not something to be terrified of, but something into which you can put all your trust without the fear of being let down or betrayed. What you have now is what you have always wanted; something to rely on – your own "Impersonal Self"!

"I can say that now you have successfully restored yourself to yourself. Through your confrontation last night, you have become self-correcting. Once you had become aware of the nature of the anomalies within yourself, you made all the necessary adjustments. As you have just been witnessing 'in yourself' you are now part of life's pleasure and your own willingness to participate in the unfolding of that life is to your credit. You will do nothing but benefit from such a position. It is up to you to enjoy such a wonderful gift. Let life reveal its secrets to you and do not place limitations on what it has to offer, for it is more than you can ever imagine – so don't bother trying. Treat each day, each moment as a blank canvas and see what picture will be created, custom made for you. Doubts and fears will never dictate to you again. They may be present, but they will be powerless! You must owe the inconvenience of their presence to your moment's hesitation before you destroyed the infinite corridor created by the mirrors. If you had delayed a fraction longer things would have been very different. But you succeeded – you have won yourself. You are an ordinary man, but a remarkable one nevertheless. You will now learn the joy of befriending those who feel the emptiness and desire for the quest which you once felt."

I felt a sudden, inexplicable melancholy.

"You will not hear me speak to you from inside you again – for now I am setting you free to discover what you can for yourself. From now on you will own your own thoughts. The idea of a friend, who has come to you as an ally and who manifests as a separate source of intelligence and remains so, is a false ideal. It has been a temporary arrangement, so that new ideas could be presented to you with as little opposition to them as possible. When I leave, you should not feel as though you are losing a part of yourself. On the contrary, as you think and speak, you will become aware that you and I are the same. You will go on to learn what there is to be learnt and enjoyed in your life.

"I have a suggestion to make. I know that you have written extensive notes describing all that has taken place in your life since you first heard my voice. There is a slight danger that you could make the mistake of going back and studying them at length in an attempt to make some sort of sense out of them. If you do, then you will only manage to entangle yourself in a philosophy, in your desire to create order through analysis. The order has already been established. It is up to you to be in step with it by remaining 'Impersonal'. If you continue to look back at what happened to you and all that has been said, and say to yourself 'those were the really good exciting times – when I was able to be with the "Impersonal" friend', your mind will start to close itself off to the present and your relationship with your life. Beware of such feelings of nostalgia! The outcome might well be that you will fail to observe how the Impersonal power can work for you – in the present. You must not look forward with a preconceived notion of how that power will manifest. It can be so subtle in the way in which it expresses itself that it might be overlooked by a mind which is not in tune with itself. You have, in a manner of speaking, been 'tuned up', or set to rights. As you so correctly observed earlier, the anomalies in your nature have been eliminated permanently. However, there is still a danger that you might feel that you have had your finest hour, and believe there are no more challenges ahead. You might become complacent. Believe me, your real journey is just beginning. The only way to familiarise yourself with the dictates of the 'Impersonal' power is to live in the world which was created by it.

"You will be in a position to perform with precision and power, and your performance has every chance of accelerating into excellence."

There was a pause. I found myself weeping.

"Do not feel sad at the loss of what you have come to know and describe as 'friend'. The final act will only be the disappearance of the distance between us. That is not something to be unhappy about. On the contrary, it is cause for celebration. You will begin to experience the never-ending understanding of yourself and the world around you. Listen to yourself as you speak – you will hear me talking. You will be a good friend to anyone you meet because you will speak a rare truth. You have become indivisible from me. Enjoy your world! Recognise that you are part of that power which, in its excitement, created a perfect expression. Your vision is now clear due to your last great efforts. What you have achieved should not be underestimated. You have thrown away those things which keep a man crouching and afraid. You are alone. You are a man in time. Do what you have to do!"

As my friend spoke as a separate entity for the last time, my anxiety subsided. I realised that the "presence" which I usually felt just prior to an encounter was right there with me and it had been ever since I had woken up. That explained my heightened state of awareness and my mood of acute appreciation. The aspect which was saying goodbye was only the "voice", the words which I had needed and apparently, I did not need anymore. I also knew that I need not feel fear now I was alone with my life, which lay before me, always mysterious – yet welcoming at the same time.

I pictured myself still standing framed in the doorway of my cabin, my head full of uplifting thoughts. My outlook was a positive one. I was not abandoned, rather the opposite, like a child once lost and afraid, that is found by its parents and is lifted into their arms. I could not define the loneliness I now felt as being cold or alienating, but a warm, full-blooded independence. I knew that what I had set out to achieve on Big Bear Mountain I had achieved. I had fulfilled the destiny which had been mapped out for me and all I could feel was a sense of completion. I was no longer "a house divided against itself", as I had once described my state of mind. I was rubbing my eyes and decided it was time for that coffee I had promised myself.

I walked down the mountain trail towards the diner. I was thinking hard, about the way I had been living my life up to now and it was clear to me that to stand up and make this change had been vital as well as inevitable. I was part of a process of evolution. I was aware and ready to respond to life's urges and was heading confidently in the direction I was meant to take. Before today, and before my first "encounter", I had been careering wildly through my life with some kind of abstract "faith" I had created for myself. It was just like closing my eyes, putting my head down and hoping for the best. Now I was holding my life up before me as a diamond of immeasurable wealth. I saw the lodge ahead of me and stopped dead in my tracks. The place seemed busy. It was then that I realised that I had not encountered a single soul for almost two weeks, not since I had picked up the keys to Cabin 12A from the attractive, but rather hard-faced woman at the reception desk on the day I had checked in. It was strange but I found myself remembering her eyes. They were large, pale green and quite hypnotic. They were the eyes of a hurt child.

I was too nervous to proceed. I automatically turned within for an answer but there was no reply. I sat down on a small boulder and waited. Nothing. The silence within me was a tranquil pool where the precious pearls of true intellect lay waiting to be discovered and brought to the surface. I was simply waiting for a pebble to be cast into that still water and release the Impersonal intellect that I had grown to love – but I was missing the point. Was I not now myself the Impersonal man, free to think, rationalise and realise for myself, through my own efforts? So I cast the stone. The answers began to bubble up like a coffee percolator. I sat while something like a hurricane raged inside my chest and head. A stream of revelations began coursing through my head – like sharp, stabbing needles, unveiling things undiscovered; opening up as yet unexplored rooms and passages, in a vast labyrinth which had been left unguarded and unattended for a long time. I was like a little dwarf of a man who had sat for the whole of his life in the porch of a great mansion, which he had never bothered to enter, so it had remained uninhabited and lifeless. Now that great house was being opened and the man who had sat outside for so long, was invited inside.

Windows and doors to an infinite number of rooms were being flung open leaving each room and passage full of sunlight and fresh air. I was dragged inside and along infinitely long corridors, struck by rippling wordless poetry and stimulated mercilessly as each separate cell in my body was lit up one by one, like a string of Christmas tree lights! Cascades of visions of unlimited potential were racing before me like an inexhaustible trail of dominoes. I was being led through myself at such close range so that I might wonder at it all. I felt an intense exhilaration as my affinity with the mundane, which I so detested, was finally broken. I imagined I heard a distant scream as some part of me fell away for ever. Eventually the winds lifted and the storm died. There was no more movement; no disturbance – and no more questions. I had finally emerged from the chrysalistic struggle from my limited self. I felt the movement of the Impersonal friend within me and for the first time, I was free to share its perception of life as if it were my own. It was full of understanding, humour and kindness. Above all there was joy – so much joy!

I had experienced an ecstasy so intense that somewhere along the line I must have momentarily blacked out. As it turned out, I had actually been sitting on that boulder, unconscious of my surroundings, for almost two hours. My fingernails were torn and ragged where I had clawed at the rock and I had dug my feet so far into the layers of mulch that they'd completely disappeared up to my calves. I had to undo my hiking boots and remove my socks in order to shake the soft, leafy soil out from them. I remained on the spot for a while, enjoying the sun in the same way that a newly hatched butterfly might sit on a leaf, waiting for its wings to dry. It was at this moment that I reached my own conclusion about writing notes. I would no longer attempt to describe the events I was experiencing. I realised that to do so would not only be utterly futile but also potentially misleading. An old friend of mine, a professional writer, had once spoken about the "disease of words". I was realising, right then and there, that I no longer needed to chronicle every thought, every realisation or revelation. It can distract from the immediate appreciation of the unfolding of one's own life. This time would be the last time. Hasn't it always been the case of attempting to describe the indescribable, communicate the incommunicable and transfer the non-transferable? After such a recent encounter with death, the only thing that mattered to me and was the reason for celebration and gratitude – was that I was alive. My taking notes, although at one time interesting and valuable, was no longer necessary. It was something that, should I pursue now, would only be out of force of habit. Watching TV regularly, when preparing for work in the mornings, and when slumping down in my armchair after returning from work, was nothing more than a bad habit. Not that there's anything wrong with watching TV – that is, if you enjoy it. For me the last thing I wanted to do was to concern myself with the lives of other people, fictional or non-fictional. Who was the man who had so diligently chronicled all that had taken place since the Impersonal friend had made himself known? He too was now a work of fiction. I was free to experience my complete self. I was no longer afraid of life, nor the world in which I lived. The hysterical and cringing half-human was dead, buried in the world between the two mirrors.

I sat cleaning myself up as much as was possible, whilst thinking about the life that lay ahead of me, which belonged to me and me alone. I had discovered that I was nobody's fool, least of all my own.

I got up from the boulder and had a good stretch – I ached all over. I had been sweating and my mouth was dry. I was hungry too. For the first time in a long time I was eager to be among people again – a bunch of strangers would be perfect. As I arrived at the lodge, I felt a brilliant smile spread across my face as I looked up at the green neon sign above the diner. It read:

<u>WELCOME!</u>
OPEN 24 HOURS
****

Epilogue

Phew! Delia ran the back of her hand across her forehead then rolled over onto her back, letting the notebook slip through her fingers onto the bedspread. Sitting still for a while, thinking and feeling absolutely nothing, she eventually decided that it was time to make a move. It came as quite a surprise to find that she had been resting for almost an hour – it had felt like ten minutes at the most.

Although she had spent the entire night reading, with the exception of forty minutes' light sleep which she couldn't avoid snatching halfway into the book, she didn't feel remotely tired (she didn't count the time she had dropped off early on, which had resulted in her nightmare). In fact she felt as though she had completely shared in the experience of the writer. She was full of optimism, energy and felt unusually exhilarated. She could detect a peculiar restlessness within her, a feeling not unlike an athlete might have before preparing himself for the hundred metre dash, or a performer hyping themselves up before walking out onto the stage. There was one thing that bothered her. Cabin 12A was a long way from being ready for anyone to occupy, but she'd deal with that later. (Had she known it, at that very moment, the people who had made the booking were phoning through a cancellation, so it was just as well that she chose not to worry). On her way home – she lived at the lodge itself, along with the resort owner and his wife – she paused at the ridge to take a look for herself at the place where the ex-occupant of 12A had finally triumphed. She hadn't quite decided yet whether what she had spent the night reading was really fact or fiction, but she had actually subconsciously accepted it as real, right from the start. One thing that she couldn't deny was that the author had referred to her as something like a "hard-faced woman" when he'd encountered her at the reception area. On the other hand, he had also mentioned that she was pretty and had made a reference to her childlike, pale green eyes. She liked that. Mind you he had been the unknown thief who had pinched the key to one of the cabins and had undoubtedly been responsible for removing the mirror from that cabin. Surely he wouldn't have gone through all that if it was just a work of fiction he was working on – and if so, why would he leave the manuscript behind?

She looked at her watch. It read 6.04 a.m. When it slowly dawned on her that she had been standing admiring yet another incredible sunset, which was forming in the eastern sky, to the right of where she was standing, she didn't feel alarmed. It did not seem remotely strange that she was witnessing a sunset at six o'clock in the morning. By the time she realised this abnormality, it had corrected itself and as she turned to walk down the mountain path, she did so accompanied by the intoxicating chorus of the woodland birds and a soft primrose yellow dawn that looked like a child's watercolour, pale and weak as if the sun were feeling lazy that morning. But life goes on, and Delia felt that she just had to get on with her day, even without the sleep she'd missed; just like that sun over there was obliged to climb the sky and light up the world. The keys to Cabin 21 and the envelope containing the cash and the apology were crammed into her back pocket. Whatever that guy had been through, he was certainly keeping up the appearance of an individual who had been through a monumental confrontation. In her mind, that deserved respect. Incidentally, she had left the notebook on the bed, completely forgetting it. Back in Cabin 12A, it was once again resting in the bedside cabinet, along with the resort guide and the Gideon's Bible.

Lightning Source UK Ltd.
Milton Keynes UK
UKOW02f1921040914

238110UK00003B/110/P